CRYPT OF THE
MOON
SPIDER

ALSO BY NATHAN BALLINGRUD

CRYPT OF THE
MOON
SPIDER

NATHAN
BALLINGRUD

NIGHTFIRE

A TOR PUBLISHING GROUP BOOK
NEW YORK

CRYPT OF THE MOON SPIDER

A Nightfire Book
Published by Tom Doherty Associates / Tor Publishing Group
120 Broadway
New York, NY 10271

www.torpublishinggroup.com

Nightfire™ is a trademark of Macmillan Publishing Group, LLC.

The Library of Congress Cataloging-in-Publication Data is available upon request.

ISBN 978-1-250-29173-8 (trade paperback)
ISBN 978-1-250-29174-5 (ebook)

Our books may be purchased in bulk for promotional, educational, or business use. Please contact your local bookseller or the Macmillan Corporate and Premium Sales Department at 1-800-221-7945, extension 5442, or by email at MacmillanSpecialMarkets@macmillan.com.

First Edition: 2024

Printed in the United States of America

0 9 8 7 6 5 4 3 2 1

TO DALE BAILEY

CRYPT OF THE
MOON
SPIDER

I.

The Barrowfield Home for Treatment of the Melancholy

Looking through the small oval window of the twin-engine passenger shuttle which carried her over the moon's gray and rubbled plains, Veronica recalled a local myth, which held that the moon was the inhabited skull of a long-dead god who once trod the dark pathways of space like a king through his star-curtained palace. Looking down upon it now, she could almost believe it. The moon seemed to exude a deathly energy, the way she imagined the bones of a holy animal might. It would not have seemed strange to see a population of ghostly horses galloping across the dusty expanse.

She craned her neck, trying to look ahead. She was eager to see the forests. Ever since she was a little girl, standing in the swaying grasses of the Nebraska plains and gazing up at the gray shadows on the moon's face, she dreamed of a day she would be able to go there to see the great woods for herself.

"Galileo thought they were oceans," she said.

Her husband shifted in the seat beside her. "Galileo what?"

He hated it when she started talking about something without reference, as though they were already in the middle of a conversation. He was a surgeon by profession—a Man of Science, he often said—and believed everything had its antecedent. She knew it was a bad habit, but she supposed it didn't matter much anymore. The bad habits would be taken away very soon.

"Nothing," she said. "Just thinking out loud."

He gave her one of his thin smiles: a compression of the lips which suggested cultivated patience, as though he were indulging a child's whims. He clasped her hand and gave it a light squeeze. "There's nothing to be afraid of."

"I'm not afraid."

But she was. She felt a curious sluggishness, a kind of separation, as though she'd become loosened from time and was jostling in its socket. She was afraid the wrong movement or word might disconnect her entirely, sending her reeling backward over the course of her own life. She did not want to live through it a second time, so she closed her eyes and thought hard about staying precisely where she was.

Her husband joined his other hand with the first, engulfing her own. "Veronica, it's true. There is nothing to fear here. It's a new beginning."

She nodded, but kept her lips clamped together. What wanted to come out was nothing she wanted to say, and nothing he wanted to hear. She tried to believe him. This was 1923, after all, not the Dark Ages. She was not coming here to have an exorcism performed. She was coming here to be cured. It was expensive and he had spent a great deal of money to give her—to give them both—this chance. She was determined to be grateful.

"It's going to be all right, isn't it?" she said.

"Of course it is, pet. Of course it is. You'll see."

"What if I can't be saved?"

He put his finger on her chin and turned her head toward him. He had his professional face on, the one he showed patients whose legs he was about to hack off. It was a face that lied. "Of course you can be saved," he said.

She turned away, looking out the window again. Then, unexpectedly, she felt the first thrill of happiness she'd known in months. "Look!"

As the shuttle sped to the night side of the moon, the forest at last appeared beneath them, stretching out in hungry miles with a deep green splendor, like the stilled waters of an ocean after all, leaves steady as stone in the unmoving air.

They flew over this expanse for several minutes, until the light from the sun winked out behind an outcropping of rock and they passed completely over to the moon's hidden face. A hard wind kicked up, buffeting their little shuttle. Her husband gripped her hand tightly; he disliked flying, and this adventure would set his dreams at a disagreeable pitch for weeks to come. She felt a flutter of delight at the thought, and stamped it out immediately.

As the shuttle sped on, the forest's character changed. A strange, white effluvium seemed to coat the trees, blowing in wispy banners in the gusting wind. At first she couldn't understand what she was looking at. Then it dawned on her that the forest was covered in a vast system of spiderwebs, cast over the canopy of every tree, so that it seemed they were flying over a ghostly wood, a revenant returned from darkness in a terrible glamor.

***

Barrowfield Home was a massive, rectangular gray building sitting among the web-shrouded trees, a great block of stone as incongruous to the setting as a sailing ship. Four stories tall and as smooth as marble, seen from on high it offered no consolation to the eye or spirit: no variation in color, no embellishment, no cheerful banner or window box of lunar perennials. It was a building constructed only to do a job, which was to warehouse people. It might as well have been a prison for criminal masterminds.

An expansive grassy clearing had been excavated from the woods out front, and as the shuttle maneuvered into landing position, Veronica saw that the space had been de-signed to accommodate outdoor activities for the patients as well as to provide a landing area for the shuttles. There was a badminton court, a small running track, and a mas-sive water fountain, along which sat a small handful of idlers. White-garbed members of the staff hovered nearby like a congregation of spirits.

Other than the grassy field, Barrowfield Home was completely enclosed by the forest. There seemed to be no way in or out of the place except by shuttle.

Her husband caught her eye and gave her a cold little smile.

The shuttle dropped abruptly. She felt a crushing wave of vertigo as it spun hard to port. The engine whined under their feet, filling the cabin with thunder. They landed with a hard jolt, snapping her teeth shut.

"Good Christ," her husband said, his face blanched.

The ground crew opened the hatch, and the cabin filled with the crashing noise of spinning rotors, the decelerating engine, and the stink of diesel. The open hatchway was a cauldron of steam and light; it looked like an artist's rendition of the entrance to Hell.

A rough-looking, heavyset man stepped aboard. His body looked pale and unfinished, like something wriggled up from the earth. Like a grub. He was smartly dressed in white-and-cream-colored clothing, creating a dissonance she found both grotesque and mildly disquieting—a worm wrapped in a gentleman's waistcoat. He limped toward them and said, "The Brinkleys, right?" His voice was coarse and uncultured, thickly Brooklyn; Veronica felt it presented a poor first impression of the Home. "My name is Charlie Duchamp." He extended his hand, but her husband only stared at it, as if he were being offered a damp tendril.

"We had a terrible commute," he said, unbuckling himself. "Your pilot flew like a Hun. Is he auditioning for a circus?"

The grub—Charlie, she reminded herself—laughed, and quickly stifled it. "Yeah, sorry about that. I'll talk to him." He turned his attention to Veronica and took her hand into his own. It was warm and dry. "You'll be staying with us awhile."

"It would seem so."

"You'll find us most accommodating. Right this way please." The words were rehearsed from a script. They sounded all wrong in his mouth.

Charlie retrieved her valise. They disembarked and he led them across the field to the Home, which hulked into the black sky. The trees walled them in, gathering darkness beneath them like heavy skirts.

Inside, the lighting was dim—"Too much light agitates the patients," the grub said—and the décor minimal. The foyer was cathedral-like, vaulting two stories overhead. Everything was made of polished moon rock, dark gray burnished to a glistening shine, like the chamber walls of an underground lake. A grand reception desk was positioned to their left, and several hallways led further into the building, disappearing into tangles of flickering shadow. White-garbed attendants occasionally moved silently from one hallway to another.

Her husband allowed himself to be guided to the receptionist's desk, where, with the scrawl of his signature, the custody of Veronica Brinkley was transferred from himself to the Barrowfield Home for Treatment of the Melancholy, where she was to be treated until sane, however long it might take.

"Do you want to meet the doctor?" Grub directed the question to her husband.

"No need. His reputation is sufficient to me. I trust he'll correspond with me when the time is right." He turned to his wife and gave her a chaste kiss on the lips. "I love you, pet. I'll see you again in no time at all." He glanced at Charlie. "Keep me apprised," he said, and then he walked briskly to the door, his footsteps echoing off the high stone walls.

Veronica suffered a wave of nausea. She closed her eyes and lowered her head, determined to keep her dignity. She heard the door open, followed by the sounds of the shuttle's rotors carving the wind. Then the door shut again, and silence engulfed her.

***

She halted at the entrance to her room. It was a cell. There could be no other word for it. The walls were carved from the same stone she'd seen in the foyer, but here the rock was dull and unpolished. A small cot—the sort you might give a housemaid—was situated in the corner. It bore one thin pillow, and the threadbare sheets were turned down in a sad imitation of a welcome. A chamber pot lurked underneath. A small chest of drawers was placed to one side, against the wall. There were no mirrors here. There were no windows.

She stepped back reflexively and was brought up short by Grub's hand pressing into the small of her back.

"I know what you're thinking," he said, his dull voice close to her ear. "But it ain't that bad. The key to Barrowfield is in here." He thumped the side of her head with one thick finger. "You can let yourself out any time."

"How?" she said. Her voice quavered, which only frightened her more.

"By letting go of your madness."

"But I don't know how." She could feel tears coming again, and this time she knew there'd be nothing she could do to stop them. She didn't want to be weak in front of such a disagreeable man, but she'd come to believe that weakness was inherent to who she was.

He dropped her bag by her feet. "That's what the doctor's for," he said. He gave her a little shove, and she stepped involuntarily into her cell. The door shut behind her, and a lock clunked heavily into place.

Veronica stood there, listening to the sound of his footsteps fading down the long hallway, until they dissipated into silence. She breathed for a moment, trying to collect herself. But it was like attempting to gather pollen in the gusting wind: she scattered like a million bright vessels. She placed her valise on the chest of drawers and carefully unpacked her clothes. Then, folding her hands into her lap, she sat on the edge of the cot. She thought she heard a voice whispering something to her.

Perhaps it was her madness, emboldened by this mad place.

***

She was left on her own for what felt like hours. During that time she lay on the cot and stared at the ceiling, letting her mind drift. She felt the advent of one of her black spells, like some strange sun threatening the horizon. A line from a simple song floated through her head, disjointed from any context she could remember. It soothed her and seemed to keep the spell at bay, so she sang the words quietly to herself.

It's all right, Moon. I love you.

And again.

It's all right, Moon. I love you.

Grub unlocked her door and swung it open. He hulked in the doorway, regarding her as she lay on the cot. His appearance seemed in accordance with the hovering black spell, as though it had summoned him from whatever dark place he lived.

"Get up," he said.

She did. She followed him obediently when he turned away and progressed down the hallway, lit from above every ten feet with bright electric lamps, bringing her eventually to the gaping entrance of Barrowfield Home. He gestured to the gardens, where she saw a few other patients scattered.

"Go play, little girl."

"When will I meet the doctor?"

"When he says. Go on."

"But how long will I have to wait? There's nothing to do! I'd like a book to read, at least."

"You'll wait until he's ready. No books. They might upset you. Either go outside or I'll take you back to your room. Your choice, girl."

"My name is Mrs. Brinkley," she said. "You knew it this morning."

His brow creased. "I thought you might want to forget that," he said.

"What, my name? Why on earth?"

"Easier that way. Now make up your mind. Last chance. I got other patients to visit."

She wanted to press him further, but more than that she wanted to avoid going back to her cell for as long as possible. So she left him at the door and wandered into the gardens. Shunning the walking paths and the badminton courts, she drifted toward the fountain, which stood against the backdrop of the forest like a great ornament of bone, the water misting in a fine, slow-drifting shower from its peak and falling into a circular pool below. Benches were arrayed around it, and she found a place on one from which she could watch the other patients milling about—men and women together, shockingly unseparated. They all wore the same drab institutional garb, the same look of hopeful disorientation—as though waiting for good news to come upon them at any moment. As more filtered from within the Home, they gathered in small, discrete pockets, hungry for some sense of familiarity or at least companionship. She counted twenty of them, give or take. Over them all, the black and star-flecked sky vaulted endlessly.

One of the men approached her. He was younger than Veronica, with disheveled auburn hair and a pleasant face that seemed somehow false, like a coat of yellow paint on a haunted house. He stopped a few feet away and smiled apologetically. "Would you like some company?"

"Please!" Veronica moved a few inches to give him room.

"You're new," the man said, sitting beside her.

"I arrived this morning. Veronica Brinkley."

"I'm Bentley Myles. I've been here two or three weeks, I think. It gets hard to tell after a while."

The name stank of money. Of course it did. No one without money could afford a stay at Barrowfield. She reminded herself once again to be grateful for her husband, who'd lifted her out of destitution.

"How long did you have to wait to see the doctor? I'm getting impatient."

"Just a day, I think. Though I'm still waiting for my first operation. Why, how long have you been waiting?"

"A few hours. I guess I'd better get used to it." She paused, unsettled. "You're having an operation?"

Bentley offered an embarrassed smile. "I'm a serious case."

"Oh." Veronica fought the urge to edge away from him, as if whatever he had might be contagious. "I'm sorry."

"I tried to kill myself."

The casual way he said it horrified her. It sounded a note inside her, like the tolling bell of a secret annihilating church buried in her heart. She glanced around, flushed with shame. "That's horrible! I—I don't know what I should say."

"It might have been all right if it was just me, but I tried to poison my wife and child, too." He looked at her, his eyes earnest. "Because I love them, you see. I love them so much. I didn't want them to suffer without a husband or a father."

Veronica did not know how to respond to this appalling revelation. Her eyes flicked to the woods surrounding them, looking for some avenue of escape.

"Anyway, I realize I was wrong. I'm looking forward to being cured." He smiled at the thought. "What about you?"

"I don't know. Nothing as serious as what you—what you're describing."

"But you're here. It must be something."

"I call them black spells. Sometimes I don't want to live."

Bentley put his hand over hers and squeezed. Her first instinct was to draw it away—it was improper, and there were people around—but it was comforting, and he seemed to intend nothing more than that. His gaze was on the trees surrounding them.

"I sometimes come out here and stare into them for hours," he said. "They're scary, aren't they?" The web-shrouded forest murmured quietly around them, dense ranks of trees gathering black air beneath their entangled arms. Bentley leaned closer, as if confiding a secret. "I've heard that sometimes patients escape into them."

"What a frightening thought." Veronica imagined escaped patients lost in the crowded acres, wandering for days, finally dying from dehydration. She imagined an uneven ring of fallen skeletons surrounding the place, marking the outer limits of their endurance. "Why would they do such a thing?"

He smiled at her. "Well. It's melancholy, I suppose."

Veronica laughed ruefully. "I suppose." And then, after a moment, "I didn't used to be this way. I was happy when I was a child. I had such grand ideas about how life would be. What happened to me? What happened to us?"

"We grew up."

They sat in silence for a little while, staring into the woods. If they could not find comfort in conversation, at least they could find it in companionship. They watched the dark, web-draped trees rustle in a sleepy wind. When Veronica closed her eyes they sounded like distant voices, or like the whispers of Galileo's imaginary sea.

Imagine a sea on the moon.

"All right you two." Grub's voice pushed through the illusion. She opened her eyes to see him standing over them. "Time's up."

II.

Dr. Cull

The following morning, she was brought to see the doctor. He was unremarkable: thin-framed, bespectacled, short black hair combed brusquely to one side, like something to be got out of the way. His clothes were unpressed and ill-fitting. He gave the appearance of someone for whom the physical responsibilities of daily life were a nuisance. Everything essential to the man resided in the cauldron of his brain, which shed a feverish heat she could almost feel.

The room—Grub called it "the Sanctuary"—was furnished like a cross between a library and an alchemist's den. The doctor sat on a large chair upholstered in red fabric. Across from him was a divan, and beside him an uncapped human skull sat on an end table, its hollow provisioned with colorful hard candies. A display shelf over the doctor's head was stocked with alembics and jars of bleached-yellow fluids. The walls were mostly covered with shelves of leather-bound books; where there were no shelves, they were decorated with star charts and anatomical diagrams. One chart in particular caught her eye. It was a carefully drawn depiction of the human brain, its various precincts labeled with handwritten notes and symbols in what she presumed was the doctor's own hand. There were no windows here, and no lamps. The only light came from candelabras situated in little alcoves throughout the room. She felt chastened by the baroque authority of the place.

He stood when Charlie ushered her in, taking her hand. "Mrs. Brinkley, I'm Dr. Barrington Cull. How lovely to meet you. Please sit down." He gestured to the divan, and she sat there a bit uncomfortably, straight-backed and proper. "Tell me, Mrs. Brinkley, have you been to a madhouse before?"

The question surprised and shamed her. She found herself unable to meet his gaze. "No. My husband will make my medical history available to you. I thought he already had."

"He has, and I've read it. You grew up in the Midwest, I understand, on a farm. Your family was of modest means but you were well cared for. When your parents died in 1913 your brothers sold the land and you moved to Boston, where you struggled with poverty until you met your husband. Is everything correct so far?"

"Yes, Doctor."

"No history of serious illness, and certainly no madhouses for you. But what I'm wondering is whether you've had cause to visit one. Perhaps you've had an unfortunate relative, or a friend who suffered from hysterics."

"No." She felt his stare.

"Nevertheless, you're afraid," he said.

"No, not really. I've read accounts. In the paper. Some of them were unsettling. But I'm sure . . ." She trailed off, because in fact she was sure of nothing at all.

Dr. Cull leaned forward on his chair. She fought a sudden instinct to recoil; she did not want to offend him. "You have nothing to fear. We don't do things the way they do on the Earth. We don't lock the mentally sick behind iron doors and corral them like livestock. We're a bit more refined in Barrowfield Home. You might think of us as surgeons of the mind."

"That's comforting, Doctor."

Dr. Cull leaned back in his chair, crossing one leg over the other. "Your husband says you have what you call 'black spells.' You become withdrawn, uncommunicative, morose without cause. You hint at suicide. He says you have failed to attend to the responsibilities of a wife. He believes such behavior is corrosive to your marriage."

Although she knew all of this, the dispassionate listing of her crimes hit her like thrown rocks, and she lowered her head. She wanted to curl into herself, and she fought hard against the impulse.

"Would you like to know a secret?" When she didn't answer, Dr. Cull proceeded anyway. "Your husband doesn't believe you're going to get better. He doesn't believe he'll ever see you again. He's left you here to wither and die."

Veronica wanted to feel stunned, she wanted to feel appalled, but this wasn't really a revelation. It only validated what she'd already suspected.

"Veronica. Look at me."

She imagined never seeing her husband's face again, never hearing his sweet voice again. The smell of his soap. The bristle of his cheek. Sadness hit her like an ax to the chest. She gasped, tried to breathe. Tears fell onto her clutched hands.

"Look at me."

With great effort, she raised her head. Whatever dreadful thing was coming her way, she wanted it. She hoped it would hurt.

Dr. Cull had left his chair and was now crouched beside the divan, staring at her with an expression she couldn't name. It was a kind of hunger, perhaps, but not the kind a man feels for a woman. Something else.

"I can help you," he said. "I can make you better."

She didn't believe him. The black spell had settled fully upon her. She'd been weak her whole life, unappreciative of the efforts others had gone to on her behalf—her father, her mother, her brothers. Her dear husband. The ungrateful, selfish sadness which had been her companion since childhood could not be removed, and she would die—she *wanted* to die—in this lonely place, far from the people she had diminished with her own wretchedness. The justice of it—the balance of it—provided its own reassurance.

In light of that, Dr. Cull's offer of a cure sounded obscene.

"I don't deserve it. My husband is right. Just lock me away. Lock the door and let me starve."

"I'll be the judge of what you deserve and what you don't.

Locking unhealthy people in cages is a barbarism which should have been abandoned long ago, along with living in caves and worshiping carved stones. We *treat* people here in Barrowfield Home, Mrs. Brinkley, and we will treat you, whether you want it or not." He paused, then stood. "Has it occurred to you that your aversion to treatment is a symptom of your illness?"

It hadn't, and the idea struck her with an almost physical impact. Here was just another case of her selfishness, of her ingratitude. The shame of it bent her over. "I'm sorry, Dr. Cull. You see what I mean. I think only of myself."

"Let me tell you a little about what we do here. Have you heard of the Alabaster Scholars?"

Veronica sat up, banking her sadness for the moment. "Yes."

"What do you know about them?"

In fact, she knew more than most. The moon had been an obsession of hers since childhood, and the Scholars in particular were a point of fascination. Long before the establishment of Barrowfield Home, in the earliest days of lunar exploration, a group of prospectors and landbreakers were said to have discovered the lair of a Moon Spider—a massive creature supposedly possessed of psychic properties— buried deep in the moon's rock. Exactly what transpired there was never reported. What is known is that the party returned to their base of operations only long enough to dismantle their rocket and transport all of the parts and stores back to the Moon Spider's lair, where they built a home for themselves in the rock.

There they tended to the Spider, protecting it from further intrusion, communing with it, studying its mysteries. They dressed in white robes resembling the vast canopies of spider silk covering the forests. Though they sometimes engaged with other miners and even the occasional pilgrim, they were reclusive and taciturn. They came to be called the Alabaster Scholars, their home referred to as a monastery.

Some speculated that there were many Spiders in many lairs spread throughout the moon.

"I know they've lived on the moon a long time. And I've read that since the Moon Spider died, they now help you instead."

"One of them does, yes. He is called Soma. You'll meet him soon. His devotion to service has thankfully continued beyond the lunar spider's death. He helps us to harness the knowledge his order cultivated over the years to aid me in my care for the afflicted, such as yourself. In this way the staff at Barrowfield helps to honor the legacy of the Moon Spider. This is important to Soma, and important to me."

"How does it work?"

"To put it simply: we reach into your brain and scoop out what's rotten. We then stitch something better into its place."

Veronica was silent. This must be the surgery Bentley had referred to. She hadn't known the specifics before coming here; only that it was radical, and celebrated for its high rate of success.

"What do you put in?"

Dr. Cull smiled. "Spider silk," he said. "The lunar silk is a remarkable neural conductor. Imagine the leper, his gangrenous flesh sloughed away, and something new—better, healthier—sewn into its place. A flesh that completely integrates with the healthy body. It's the same thing."

She imagined herself walking through Boston again, arm in arm with her husband and untroubled forevermore by the black spells. Her mind stitched together by moon filaments. A quiet thrill glided through her blood, as though she had been wandering lost through a dark wood and stumbled upon an honest-to-God gingerbread house.

"It sounds too good to be true," she said.

"Well of course, there is the occasional complication. Treating the insane is not a game for children, and it does not adhere to the brute formulae of your husband's profession. What I do here is revolutionary. There is risk, yes. But it's minimal. And I think you'll agree, it's justified."

"Does my husband know this is what you're going to do?"

"Your husband has remanded you to my care. What he knows or does not know is of no concern to me. As I said, he does not expect to see you again. We shall surprise him."

Veronica said nothing. For the first time in many years, she began to feel hope.

"Well." Dr. Cull leaned back his chair. His demeanor abruptly changed, all sense of intimacy fading away. It was as though an office door had been closed. He was simply a doctor again: a cold function, a knife held at the ready. "We'll begin tomorrow. In the meantime, Charlie will escort you back to your room."

Grub's hand fell on her shoulder. She'd forgotten he was there.

***

Deep morning on the Nebraska farm. Ten-year-old Veronica lay on her bed, the windows open and a cool breeze belling the curtain, carrying the woody smell of the wheat field into the house. In a few hours the air outside would fill with light, with the voices of her father and brothers—their easy, rough talk an assurance that the world still moved according to its prescribed rhythms. She would be in the kitchen with her mother, preparing breakfast, preparing for the day's chores. She had a fine life, defined by hard work and by the drawing forth of good fortune from a bountiful earth.

But for now the sky was dark, and it was hers.

She eased out of bed and climbed down the ladder from her loft. Her parents slept beneath her, their bodies warm under the covers, as reliable and solid as the earth. She tiptoed past, careful to avoid the parts of the floor that creaked, and slipped out the front door.

The sky was always vast in Nebraska, but at night the scope of it staggered the mind. The stars were bright and thick, like a rime of frost, ballooning along the rim of the Earth in an opaque smear which her father told her was the galaxy. He'd perched her on his shoulders one night when she was very small, shirking their evening chores with an exhilarating wickedness, and pointed out characteristics of the night sky to her, including the little vessels that streaked like meteors on their way to and from the moon.

He pointed at the moon and said, "Do you see those dark smudges there? Those are forests."

She had never seen a forest in her life, but her mother told her stories about them. They were filled with wolves and witches' huts.

"Are they scary, Daddy?"

"No, Piglet. They're not scary. They're just far away."

"I want to go."

"Oh, you do? How are you gonna get there?"

"In one of the slippery lights."

"You mean those streaks of light?" She could hear the smile in his voice. "Those are moon rockets."

"Rockets," she said, trying out the word. It felt sharp and strong.

"Maybe one day you just might, Piglet. I suspect you got a few surprises in you. Why do you want to go there?"

"Because it looks sad. It's all alone."

Her father reached above him and placed one big hand across her back, patting her gently. "Maybe if you sing it a song it won't feel so lonely."

"What song should I sing?"

"How about you make one up. Just for the moon."

"Will it hear me?"

"I believe it will, Piglet."

So she thought about it, and made up a little lullaby. She sang it quietly, because she was embarrassed. But it felt too important to let that stop her.

Moon, are you lonely?

Are you cold?

It's all right, Moon.

I love you.

You can live with me.

Now, standing by herself underneath the sky, she was surprised it came back to her, and she sang it again, this time even more quietly. But that was all right: the moon could hear her even when she whispered.

***

Dr. Cull sat on the other side of the room, one leg crossed over the other. His eyes flicked between her and the notebook he was writing in. She lay back on a divan, foggy with sleep. The lighting was low—a few candelabras situated in little alcoves built into bookshelves. There were no windows; only light, knowledge, and warmth. Veronica felt more at peace here than she had anywhere since the farm.

"Did you dream?" His voice was quiet and soothing.

"Yes."

She didn't remember falling asleep. The doctor had offered her tea, and then that was all.

The hint of a memory tugged at her thoughts. She peered into an unlit corner on the far side of the room and saw a white shape standing there, a ghost in shadows.

An Alabaster Scholar.

Soma. It stood so still she thought it might be a statue, or a figment. But she knew it was neither.

"Tell me what you dreamt."

With effort she turned her attention to the doctor. If he was bothered by her distraction, he did not show it.

"I dreamed I was waking up on the farm, when I was little. I sneaked outside before anyone else was awake and looked at the night sky."

"Why did you have to sneak?"

"I didn't have to. I just did. I didn't want to wake my parents."

"Would they have been angry with you?"

"No."

"You're certain of this?"

She paused. She was, wasn't she? "Yes."

Dr. Cull scribbled some notes. "What is it about the sky that fascinated you?"

"The moon."

He nodded as he wrote. "Of course. The moon. The siren of the night. Tell me about her."

The doctor's characterization surprised Veronica. She took a moment to process it. He called it *her*. How strange that a man of science would indulge in sentimentality.

How to quantify what it meant to her? "The moon is . . . beautiful."

He scoffed. "Banality. Don't evade me, Mrs. Brinkley."

The rebuke hurt. She fought an impulse to withdraw, knowing it would only further disappoint the doctor. So she considered what she really meant. "When I was little I thought about it all the time. I watched the ships go back and forth in streaks, far away. I imagined going there myself." She laughed self-consciously. "I worried about the moon. I even made up a little lullaby for it. I'd forgotten, until coming here."

She found herself staring at the Scholar again: still un-moving, still shrouded in shadow. She could feel its gaze brushing her skin like feathers.

"Sometimes, when it was very bright, it hurt. I could feel its light in my head."

"Interesting." He made more notations in his book. "Of course you know of the relationship between the moon and madness."

"I know there's meant to be one."

"Not meant to be. Is. And I can deduce from what you tell me that madness has been gestating in your mind since you were very young, Mrs. Brinkley. One might call it des-tiny, were one disposed to talk nonsense."

This information devastated her. "Then there's no hope for me."

"I don't know what it means, just yet. Perhaps not the limitations you fear. Perhaps, instead . . . fresh possibilities."

"What do you mean?"

Dr. Cull studied her silently. After a moment he rang a small bell on the table by his side, summoning Charlie into the room. "That will be all for now, Mrs. Brinkley. I'll fetch you once I've had time to consider our options."

Charlie appeared by her chair.

"Dr. Cull?" she said. When he did not respond she looked toward the Scholar, as if it might step from its dark corner and dispel her confusion with a quick explanation. But it was no longer there. Where had it gone? And when?

Without looking up from his notebook, the doctor said, "Mr. Duchamp, please escort her back to her room."

***

She was not let out of her cell for several days. Grub came by twice daily to deliver her meals, and at first she was quiet and meek, asking when the doctor might see her again, accepting his silence as a deserved retort for the selfishness of the question. Of course Dr. Cull had other patients to see, surely some with better prospects for recovery than her own; why would she think she was entitled to his time? She consoled herself with the thought of Bentley getting better under his care. Perhaps he could return to his family and settle into the role of a responsible husband and father, the way he was meant to.

But on the fourth or fifth day—it was hard to keep count—her patience cracked. She pleaded with Grub, and when he still did not relent she demanded he tell her why the doctor was ignoring her. She slung the food tray away, splashing it against the wall. Grub was indifferent. He left her with the mess until she was finally unable to bear the stink of it and cleaned it up herself, using one of her own shirts as a rag.

Worse than the lack of answers, worse even than Dr. Cull's apparent abandonment of her, was Grub's own unimpeachable silence. Not a word of explanation, not even a sneering dismissal. He moved into and out of her room twice each day like a mechanical man, designed to fulfill its basic function and not a single thing more.

Finally, a dark spell found her again. She was surprised it had taken so long. It didn't come on suddenly; rather, she only became aware of it once she was fully in its grip.

She had a sense of slowly falling, more a drift than a plummet. She started speaking when she was alone, soothing herself by speaking aloud her thoughts as if someone else was in the room to hear her, then whispering curses upon Grub, Dr. Cull, her husband. She indulged fabulous dreams of shocking and brutal revenge, dreams which she would never reveal to another soul and which would plague her with guilt in her lucid state. After a few more days the anger turned inward, as it always did. She spoke to herself with a cruel logic: *Of course the doctor won't see you anymore, you're incurable. Why would he waste time on someone like you. Everyone who knows you eventually becomes disgusted with you.* These statements were unassailable because they were bolstered by all the evidence at hand. If they were lies, as she sometimes tried to tell herself, then they wouldn't have been proven again and again.

Finally, she stopped speaking altogether. If silence was to be her lot then she would embrace it. She found it cold at first, but by the middle of her second week in isolation it had become calming, something warm she could wrap around herself. She no longer spoke to Grub when he delivered her food, and when he broke routine one day by taking her sheets and her dirty clothes to wash, even the ones she was wearing, she simply stood impassively, utterly indifferent. When he was finished, he stood in the middle of the room for a moment, the soiled items gathered in his arms, and watched her. It was not a lascivious stare; it seemed instead that he wanted her to say something.

If he did, he left disappointed.

When he returned with her items clean, she would not change into them. Better to be naked, she thought, like the animal I am.

On the night before everything changed, she heard the lullaby in her sleep. Not the child's doggerel she had written herself, but the meandering, unmelodic tune she had set it to. She dreamed of a black gulf. Something swam in its depths, just beyond her sight.

***

The door slid open. Grub stood in the frame. "Time for another session."

She didn't respond to him. She didn't even move. It was breakfast time but she wasn't hungry. His voice sounded sharp and upsetting, like a dropped plate in church.

"Get up, girl. If you don't come on your own I'll drag you out by your ankle. Makes no difference to me."

After a moment, she stood and dressed while Grub waited. He led her down a series of hallways and up two flights of stairs to the Sanctuary, where Dr. Cull was waiting for her, sitting in his soft chair, couched by the low warm lamplight. The Alabaster Scholar stood in the corner, as before. She took her seat. All the anger she had banked over the past several days started to dissipate, replaced by a simpering gratitude which she loathed herself for feeling.

"Thank you for seeing me, Doctor." Her voice seemed alien.

He gestured to the cup at her side. "Have some tea."

A lavender-scented steam coiled from within. She hesitated. "Will it be like last time?"

"If you mean will it facilitate the work in our session to-day, yes."

She drank.

***

Deep morning on the Nebraska farm. Ten-year-old Veronica lay on her bed, the windows open and a cool breeze belling the curtain, carrying the woody smell of the wheat field. In a few hours the air outside would fill with light, with the voices of her father and brothers—their easy, rough talk an assurance that the world still moved according to its prescribed rhythms. She would be in the kitchen with her mother, preparing breakfast, preparing for the day's chores. She had a fine life, defined by hard work and by the drawing forth of good fortune from a bountiful earth, and so it was with terror and disbelief that she contemplated fetching an ax from the barn and swinging it into the sleeping skulls of her family.

The thought crawled out of the wet black loam of her brain like some horrid new insect. It scrabbled unchecked through her mind, eating everything clean and good in her, laying clutches of wet, mucousy eggs in its stead.

She coiled into herself. She felt vile. She pressed her face into the pillow and held it there, hoping to smother her-self. No child with such thoughts deserved to live. But pain tightened her chest and she pulled away at last, heaving in the sweet-smelling air, damning herself for her lack of re-solve. She would continue to live because she was weak.

She eased out of bed and climbed down the ladder from her loft. Her parents slept beneath her, their bodies frozen in what appeared to be attitudes of struggle. Their stillness contained a suggestion of just-finished violence she had never noticed before, and she felt an exotic sort of shame. She turned her eyes from them and crept out the front door, moving quickly so the cold air wouldn't wake them.

The sky was always vast in Nebraska, but tonight it was a starved emptiness, the full moon crackling with energy. She knew there was no up or down in space, and as she stared into the darkness she felt that she might fall into it, rising from the earth like one of the slippery lights into an infinite abyss.

Behind her came her father's voice. "Do you see those dark smudges? Those are forests."

She turned. The Scholar, Soma, stood where she expected her father to be, white robe radiant in the moonlight, billowing in the gusting wind. Its cowl was pulled low, showing only a long pale chin.

"That is where the Moon Spiders live."

"They're dead," she whispered. "They're all dead."

"Yes."

She looked at the moon again, the words of her lullaby perched on her tongue. When she looked back, Soma was gone and she was alone under the sky. She was gratified to find the ax in her hand, its head in the dirt by her feet, moonlight riding its hungry edge.

***

Veronica opened her eyes to see Dr. Cull smiling down at her. A bright light was affixed to the ceiling somewhere behind his head, providing him a hot, garish halo. His breath was rank; she pulled back slightly, her head pressing into a pillow. This caused a distant pulse of pain to course down her spine, and she gasped. As awareness of her body came back to her, like a flurry of telegraphs arriving over the wire, she also became aware of her surroundings. She was no longer in the Sanctuary. She was strapped to a gurney in a dark, cavernous room. Light shed from three bright lamps suspended above. She was cold; a thin white sheet covered her body. A larger sheet was stretched tightly just above the level of her eyes, like a wall isolating the top of her head.

She was in an operating room.

Dr. Cull put a hand on her shoulder. "Don't move, Mrs. Brinkley. You're doing very well. Just remain still."

"Where am I?"

"You're in the treatment room. There's nothing to fear."

"I don't remember getting here." She sensed other presences in the room, though she could only see the doctor. Shadows moved across the ceiling, shifting like the shoulders of huge men. Standing behind her. She tried to turn her head to see, and the pain came back, more sharply this time, yet still oddly removed—like a raised voice in a distant room. One of the shadows jerked, and she felt her head held firmly in place by something.

"I must insist you remain still," said Dr. Cull. "You risk injury to yourself."

"What's happening to me?"

Cull smiled again, though she could tell his patience was thinning. A sheen of perspiration gleamed on his forehead. "I told you. You're being treated, as we discussed. You were given a sedative in your tea. You may feel disoriented for some time, as it was quite strong. Smaller doses have been known to wear off before we're quite finished. I think you'll find the disorientation preferable."

"I had a dream. It was so bad." Simply acknowledging it brought a flood of horror. She felt tears slide down the side of her face, tickling her ears. She forced herself not to try to wipe them away. She wanted to be still for the doctor. She wanted to do what she was told.

He leaned in closer, his fetid breath spilling over her again. He studied her face impassively: a carpenter examining a beam. "That was not a dream, Mrs. Brinkley. That was a memory."

"No." She shook her head. She couldn't control herself; it was a visceral reaction. There was no pain this time, though. The shadows on the ceiling were gone, the light unoccluded and strong. "No it wasn't."

Dr. Cull regarded her for a moment, his expression kindly but stern. "I know it seems shocking, but this is not unusual. The mind is very complicated. It's like a labyrinth. It can even deceive itself. Memories you thought were yours are sometimes fabrications, constructed to protect you from the truth. Discovering what's real is often a traumatic experience. But it's the first step in repairing your brain. In making you well."

"Soma was there."

A shadow of concern passed across the doctor's face. "You're mistaken. You're confusing what you saw in your mind with Soma operating on you."

"No. He was there. You did something to me." Her body was shuddering; something cold nested inside her. "You're a liar." Later, the memory of this accusation would appall her. But now, if she could have mustered the energy, she would have spat in his face.

He reacted as though she had done just that. He withdrew quickly, his disgust plain. "That's rude behavior, Mrs. Brinkley." Looking over her head at someone standing behind her gurney, he said, "Take her to her room."

As she was wheeled away, she caught a glimpse of the surgical drape sheet that had been stretched taut around her head. The Alabaster Scholar stood still against the wall behind it. He did not watch her leave. Blood coated his hands, and his robes were stained with it, like a child's bib. Then the door shut, and she watched the lightbulbs strung along the stone ceiling slide by as her escort wheeled her down a long hall. She was exhausted; time abstracted itself. Finally she was deposited back in her own room.

Someone—Grub, she suspected—had placed a hand mirror on her bureau. Looking into it, she discovered that her head had been shaved. The shock of it almost made her cry out. Her naked face loomed from the mirror, swollen and obscene. Crowning her bare scalp was a row of fat, ugly stitches, the skin around them pink and irritated. Fingerprints of blood were smeared around them, the signature of a shoddy craftsman. She heard a strange sound—a kind of keening. She thought at first that it emerged from the fissure in her head, like some essential air whistling away. But soon she recognized the sound of her own grief. She took some comfort from it. Grief, at least, was familiar.

***

Later, she was brought into the courtyard again, where she found herself mingling with a different group. There were fewer patients here—less than a dozen—and all had shaven heads with crowns of stitches. They looked like they were wearing absurd hats. Where there had been an attitude of hope and anticipation in the first group, these people roamed the garden in listless ambulations.

Bentley was here, and Veronica joined him on a bench. They faced away from the home, turning instead to the dark forest. Bentley looked wan, almost ghostlike. Though younger than Veronica, he had aged since the last time they'd seen each other. The stubble of hair along his scalp shone silver when it caught the light. The seam around his head was swollen and irritated. He scratched compulsively at the stitches over his left ear; a few had come loose.

For a while they didn't speak. They just watched the forest together, listening to the quiet rustle of leaves in the mild wind. Veronica turned the last session over in her mind, reliving the dream, wondering if Dr. Cull could possibly be right. Could she have harbored those thoughts about her family? Had she carried an ax into her own home? Each time, she rejected the idea. It was impossible.

Then what was happening? Why did he insist it was real?

They might have passed their full allotment of leisure time this way, each lost in their own labyrinth, but Bentley finally broke the silence. "He's not helping us."

The pronouncement fed the cinder of unease she was trying to snuff out. "Don't say that."

Bentley stared into the woods. "Do you get headaches?" He plucked at the loose stitches over his ear again, provoking a small trickle of blood.

Reflexively, Veronica touched the stitches around her own head. "No. Bentley, I wish you wouldn't do that."

"I woke up in the middle of the process. Did I tell you?"

Veronica felt cold. "No."

"Dr. Cull was screaming at someone. Someone standing by my head. But the funny thing is, I wasn't looking out of my own eyes. I was looking at my body from somewhere else."

"Maybe you had an astral experience. I've heard the soul can—"

"No. It was from behind a glass on the shelf. A few feet to one side. Like I was in a jar. I don't think he had any idea I was awake. There was blood on the floor. That big one was there, the one who always takes us to our rooms."

"I call him Grub," Veronica said. She felt a thrill of danger saying the name aloud.

Bentley did not react. "I think, soon, I'm going to run for the forest." He sounded far away.

"No. No, don't."

"They're doing bad things to us, Veronica."

The trees stood like cold sentinels, crowded and bleak, curtained with webs. Veronica thought about the rumors of other patients who'd fled into the woods. When first hearing of them, she'd wondered what could have driven them to such a suicidal act. Now, the idea had a dangerous appeal. What if they hadn't all died? What if, instead, they were living wild, like characters in an Edgar Rice Burroughs novel, moving through the forest as easily as ghosts through an empty mansion? What if they found a city of living Moon Spiders, where madness was a holy marker, and they were received as prophets?

But she said, "You can't go out there. I know it seems confusing but Dr. Cull is trying to help us. He'll fix you and when you go back home they'll see you're better, and you can go back to your family. They'll see what happened wasn't your fault."

"I know it wasn't my fault. I just didn't want to live. You can't make somebody want to live." He pulled absently at the loose stitches over his ear, and she watched in horror as a spider the size of her fingernail wriggled out.

Around them, other patients were starting to drift back inside. Staff members ushered them along. Soma stood by the door, a tall white figure who shone amidst the gray rabble of the mad. Here to take someone into session, no doubt.

"It's time to go back inside, Bentley. Please."

"All right." He rose and, for now, turned his back on the forest. They joined the shuffling throng. Veronica paused once she came abreast of the Scholar, but it did not pull her out of line. Disappointed, she continued inside with the rest.

***

That night, Grub let himself in after a brief knock, carrying her dinner tray. There was a plate of cold meat covered with a pale gravy, along with some stirred greens and a glass of milk. She accepted the tray and placed it on the bureau beside her bed. When she did not hear the door close again behind her, she turned back, cold trickles of fear rolling through her body.

Grub still stood there, a hulk in the door frame. A lamp flickered behind him, pushing his shadow into her room. The heavy features of his face looked like mounds of clay. A crescent of light glistened in one eye.

"Thank you," she said, careful to keep her voice even. And then, absurdly, as though she were dismissing a servant, "That's all."

"I heard you today. In the garden."

So he crept about like a child and listened to other peoples' conversations. She suppressed a shudder. "Eavesdropping is impolite," she said. She felt the bureau pressing into her back.

"I'm not a polite man."

She had nothing to say to this, so she waited.

"I heard what you called me."

She did not remember speaking of him at all. What would she have said? She only remembered trying to galvanize Bentley's spirits.

And the forest. The patient allure of the forest.

"'Grub,' you said."

She felt dizzy. "Charlie—Mr. Duchamp. I'm sorry. I didn't—"

"Did you mean it like a mealworm? Or do you mean I'm dirty?"

"I don't know what I meant. I'm so sorry." She couldn't keep the tremor from her voice anymore. She felt as though she stood at the edge of a terrible precipice.

"Which did you mean," he said.

Veronica stared at her feet. A tear fell and spattered on her shoe.

"You remembered an ax." His voice was closer now; he had stepped into her room. Her breath caught and she looked up at him. He had come into the radius of her own small candle. She could see his face clearly now. There was an intensity there, but it did not look like anger.

"Yes," she said.

"Did the priest give it to you?"

"I don't—I don't know what you mean."

"The spider priests are scurrying in their tunnels. Can't get them all. Can't ever get them all. But I like to try."

The spider priests? "The Alabaster Scholars," she said. So there were more.

"Yes. They're all agitated. More than usual." He stepped closer. She had nowhere to go. She turned her face away. She felt his breath on her cheek. "They know you. How?"

"Please. I don't know what you're talking about."

He remained there another moment, the stink of dried sweat rooting into her nostrils. Then he retreated to the door. "I like it if it's a mealworm," he said. "Mealworms turn into beetles."

He left, closing the door after him.

She ate her dinner and left the tray by the door. It took her a long time to go to sleep. When she did, she dreamed that a Scholar stepped out of a shadow in the corner. It watched her for a long time, its robes fluttering in the wind.

Not wind. There was no wind in here. Spiders, hundreds of them, crawling beneath.

When it opened its mouth to speak, she heard her mother's voice.

III.

The Alabaster Scholars

She dragged the ax along the ground behind her, making a furrow in the dirt. The farm house was tiny against the star-dappled sky and against the wheat fields, rippling gently in the dark of the morning, as if something unseen had passed through them. Other than the barn to her left, there was nothing else to break her line of sight. She felt like an insect walking across the thin shell of the world. The slightest breeze might send her spinning into the endless night. If she was quick enough, she might grab the sickle of the moon before she was lost. Or she might choose to keep her hands carefully clasped and watch the moon drift by untouched. She might choose what lived in that darkness instead—the gods who strode the unlit avenues, the intelligences radiating from black fathoms.

When she reached the front door, it opened quietly. The

interior was darker than the outside; none of the moon's light drifted through. Hefting the ax in both hands now, she navigated a confident path among the chairs and the table, the butter churn and the pot-bellied stove. She could pluck out her own eyes and be as sure of her step.

They would wake soon. She had to be fast.

Her parents remained splayed in their reckless attitude, and she stood over them for a moment, letting the shame of their vulnerability pass through her like a hot wind. She considered the order of procession, and decided it must be her mother first. Her father would wake up and hesitate. He would burn a crucial second disbelieving what his own eyes told him. He still believed in the essential weakness of women.

Her mother knew better.

Afterward, the boys would be easy.

***

Veronica awoke to her own screams. She was pulling against her restraints, her body mobilizing before her conscious mind surfaced. This time she was not greeted by Dr. Cull's calm, curious face, and she kept thrashing, unable to bring herself under control. Another noise—unrecognizable at first—filled the treatment room. A rage-filled, grunting, teeth-gnashing snarl of anger and invective ran counterpoint to her own cries. Shadows lunged and shuddered on the ceiling, cast by the lamplight behind her.

"Stop him! Hack it off!" Dr. Cull's voice.

A remote part of her brain understood she was panicking. She tried to employ the deep-breathing exercises Dr. Cull had taught her, she tried to still her body, but she could do neither. She had no control. She stared down at her hands, watched them clutch repeatedly as though grasping for something, utterly independent of her will. A vertiginous horror filled her, and she gave herself over to the screams.

Orderlies rushed into the room, flowing past her and disappearing behind the drape sheet over her head. She felt the stab of a needle somewhere above her eyeline, and within moments the panic receded behind a euphoric rush of warmth. Her cries became a startled gasp of joy. She felt suddenly as if she were gliding along warm thermals, the world of her youth a beautiful patchwork below.

Her horror remained, though, muffled and isolated. Even this happiness was a manipulation.

She smiled at the orderlies as they hustled about the room, and when she saw Dr. Cull emerge from behind the sheet, his face blood-dappled and ruddy with anger, she tried to reach for his hand, her happiness at the sight of him uncontainable. The restraints foiled her, so she contented herself with repeating his name, enjoying the roll of sylla-bles over her tongue. Enjoying the simple happy presence of him.

Two orderlies dragged Soma out from behind the screen, struggling. Its right arm was severed at the elbow. Grub stood with them, breathing heavily, a bloody hatchet clutched in his right hand. They departed the room, leaving a gory trail behind. Veronica suppressed a laugh.

All of it transpired in near silence. Not a word was spo-ken between Dr. Cull and the orderlies, and it wasn't until they were gone that he finally approached her, his face still locked in an anger just now beginning to recede. When he leaned over her, she felt something akin to holy wonder.

"You're all right, Mrs. Brinkley." To someone outside her view, he said, "Is it too late?"

What a silly thing to say, she thought, and she laughed. "Of course I'm all right, Doctor!"

He looked irritated. "Please don't talk. It's very annoying."

The rebuke stung, but her happiness was unaffected. Something buried in her mind struggled without effect. "All right, Doctor." Realizing she had just spoken, she laughed again. "Whoops! Sorry."

Dr. Cull wrenched aside the sheet suspended behind her. "If you insist on talking I will have an orderly suture your mouth closed until you are returned to your room."

An orderly standing behind her said, "I can't get it out."

"We'll have to burn it out then."

For the first time, she noticed a mirror on the ceiling; it revealed the scene behind her. A small wooden table held a burning lantern, densely inscribed charts, and a strip of unrolled leather displaying a bloody scalpel alongside an array of more esoteric surgical instruments. The rounded cap of a human skull rested upside down beside them, like a finger-bowl in a cannibal's drawing room. The stitches around her head had been undone, the surrounding flesh peeled back and clamped down. She saw the pale gray curve of her own brain breaching the skull. She watched as a spider stepped gingerly across its surface. Long fibrous strands trailed from her brain to the floor, where they ended in a bloody swamp.

"Oh, Doctor," she said, unable to contain a surge of euphoria, cascading with a raw and terrible energy through her body. "It's so beautiful." Cold tears trailed down the sides of her face. Something broken barked and howled behind her joy.

"I did warn you," said Dr. Cull. He called a name over his shoulder, and an orderly appeared with a needle and catgut.

***

Her father hoisted her onto his shoulders, and together they walked out into the wheat. She tilted her head back so all she could see were the stars, sliding above her in a glittering stream. The moon was so bright it almost crackled.

"Some people say the moon is a skull," her father said.

"That's not true."

"That's a corpse up there, shining so prettily in sky."

Veronica didn't like that thought. She put her hands over her father's mouth.

***

The next several minutes passed in a fog. She remembered the orderlies pulling the stringy webs from her brain; the hideous joy she'd been prisoner to snapped like a cut string as the webbing was yanked free, and she would have screamed again had she been able to open her mouth. She remembered an orderly affixing the top of her skull back into place and sealing it with an unguent scooped from a jar with thick, blood-speckled fingers. Her scalp tugged back into place like a cap, the needle and thread pulling it tight, lifting her eyebrows. She remembered Dr. Cull observing from a small distance, his face a study in—anger? Fear?

Then the lights stuttered, surged, and went out. The darkness was absolute. Veronica flashed back to the feeling she'd had on the farm while staring into the sky, and for an ecstatic moment she thought it had finally happened, she'd fallen from the surface of the world and gone tumbling into space.

Dr. Cull barked an order, dissolving the illusion. A dim light flared, and orderlies surrounded her, one holding aloft a candelabra with three smoking tapers.

"They've cut power!" someone said.

"Get her to her room. Lock everything down. Send Charlie to me."

They wheeled her into the dark hallway. Distant shrieks and screams echoed around her, the panicking patients locked in their lightless cells. The orderlies lit their way with candles. Normally she marked the passage to her room by counting the islands of light left by the hanging lamps; there were twenty-four between the treatment room and her cell. But with the lights out, she had no markers. So she did not know how far they'd gone when the lead orderly cried out. Figures rushed them from both sides—white, ghostly shapes lurching from the shadows like angry spirits, as if they'd emerged from the walls themselves. The shadow of a raised arm clutching a knife swung across the ceiling. Shrieks of fear and pain broke around her.

Someone shouted, "Put her out!" and the orderly at her head leaned over her, eyes wild and face glistening with sweat, frantically preparing a syringe. A blade from behind opened his throat, dousing her face with hot blood before he could finish.

His body fell onto the gurney and tipped her over, slamming her face onto the stone floor. Her left arm wrenched painfully as the ties around her wrists held, pulling against the bone. Her body was partially suspended from the gurney, her eyes clouded with the orderly's blood. She tried to shout but the stitches pulled taut, sending a sharp spike of pain through her head. She wondered if the top of her skull had been knocked loose, imagined it rolling like a dropped coin down the hallway.

A wave of nausea passed through her, and she closed her eyes, breathing deeply, concentrating on keeping it in check. She did not want to vomit with her mouth sewn shut.

After a moment, the feeling receded to something dull and manageable. The sounds of the scuffle had stopped. She felt the orderly's blood on her face, grown cool and sticky, and she started to shake with a violent fear. She couldn't apprehend what was happening to her. It was too thorough, too complete a horror, as though the feeling had itself become something physical, wrapped around her bones. Something that could not be removed from her without splitting her open like a slaughtered pig.

An image struck her: her own father, stalking these lunar halls with a dead sow hooked over his shoulders, shirt soaked with its blood. Looking for her. A dark intent roosting in his brain.

She cast a terrified glance down the hallway, sure she

would see him there. Three or four of the dropped candles had stayed lit, and they glimmered on the floor like fairie lights. Something large lay in a heap among them several feet away, but she couldn't crane her neck enough to make out what it was.

They're doing bad things to us, Veronica.

She tried to call through the stitches, a guttural moan filling the passage. No voices were raised in response. There were no hurried footsteps. She heard only her own strained breath.

The gurney had been damaged when it fell over. She strained her left arm, rattling the metal bar in its berth. She rolled her body away from it as far as she could, throwing all her strength into dragging her arm after her. She groaned; the pain in her wrist and shoulder was immense. The bar snapped abruptly and slammed into the wall near her face.

She unstrapped her right wrist, then her feet. Finally she released her left wrist, swollen and raw, from the broken bar. She curled onto the floor, her whole body bruised and aching. A ginger touch to her scalp reassured her that her skull was still intact. She waited for the tears to come, but discovered she had neither the energy nor the patience for them. Instead, she used the wall to pull herself upright, and she assessed her surroundings.

The heap lying beneath the light some distance away was another orderly. He was dead: his body twisted halfway around, his skull crushed. A pool of blood shone blackly around his head like an underground lake. Remembering the stitches, Veronica clamped a hand around her mouth, willing herself not to cry out.

Behind her, nearer to the toppled gurney, was the orderly whose throat had been cut as he tried to sedate her, whose blood she wore all over her face. She thought there had been a third, but there was no sign of him now. Nor of their attackers: Scholars. Several of them.

In both directions the hallway disappeared into darkness. Shallow recesses marked the locations of occasional doors. She approached the nearest one and tried the handle, but it was locked. Electing not to pass the crushed orderly, she went in the other direction, one hand trailing along the wall for support.

She wanted to go back to her room.

But

he sewed my mouth shut.

In a day layered with horrors, this one only now began to impress itself upon her. Cull did this. Not her husband, not Grub. Cull. The man she had given her faith to. The man her husband had signed her over to. This was not an example of unorthodox procedures meant to make her well, nor was it the application of strange lunar technology. This was a vicious and petty thing that he had done to her. A casual brutality.

Anger flickered in the back of her brain, mounting to a steady, hot radiation. By its new light she could see her own past in ways previously concealed from her. By whom? By Dr. Cull? By her husband? By her father, even? At the thought of him, she had a flash of memory: her mother's face, beads of sweat on her forehead from the work she performed, watching her with a strange mix of frustration and sorrow. She was trying to tell her something.

The hallway terminated at a closed door. This one was unlocked. She pushed it gently open, peering into a candlelit gloom.

A stairway descended steeply between rough-hewn walls. A bank of thick tallow candles flared and spat from candelabras placed on either side of the door, crackling as the air from the hallway washed over them. Veronica closed the door behind her and took one of the candelabras from its place. Moved by anger as much as by curiosity, she crept slowly down the stairs. Blood dotted the stone steps like a trail of breadcrumbs. The candlelight slid over the jagged rock in bright panes and pooled shadows, so that it looked like she was moving down a passageway made from shards of glass. An occasional gust of cold air rolled up from the darkness below and guttered the flames on their wicks.

A sound fluttered from somewhere ahead: a shuffling, furtive noise, like an insect squeezing itself into a crack in the wall. She froze, the recklessness of her behavior suddenly apparent to her. But the thought of turning back, of willingly delivering herself back into the care of the institution, was untenable. A dreadful epiphany: it would be better to die. She took a moment to gather her resolve and started down again, following the candlelight painted on the wall.

The stairs rounded a corner, and she came upon an Alabaster Scholar splayed on the stone, crawling downward. Not Soma—another one. Its bloody robes were filthy and torn. It paused when the light reached it, turning its head to look at her. She could read no expression there.

"Help me," it said.

It did not speak to her in her own language. It was something alien, sibilant and musical, chiming through her mind, igniting lamps long dark. It did not speak any language known on Earth, as far as she knew, and yet she understood it.

The realization sent an involuntary shiver of disgust through her. That she should somehow recognize the speech of this creature appalled her beyond reason. She imagined its pallid fingers weaving spider webs into her brain, and she had an impulse to touch the candle flames to its robes and kick it down the stairs in a pinwheel of fire.

Instead she walked past it, continuing her own descent. Its fingers brushed her ankle. She left it behind, to crawl through darkness alone.

Time passed in the burning of tallow and the hot drippings of wax onto her hand. The candles had diminished to half their height when she began to notice irregularities in the steps, like ripples. She knelt to inspect one and found a root, thick and gnarled, had burst through the rock. More became apparent as she descended further, where they had breached the walls or crumbled stairs to rubble. She picked her way around them with care.

Finally, the long descent ended. She emerged into a room which opened before her like a narrow tomb. The candle shed a weak light, but it was enough to see more bodies on the ground. Three at least, strewn along a narrow aisle between what looked like wooden pews. More Scholars, hacked to death. The roots of trees rose through the rubbled stone in great black arcs. She had to push her way through spiderwebs as she moved through the room, the flame from her candles igniting them in sporadic, bursting clouds of light.

As she picked her way between the pews and over the bloody corpses, an altar swam up through the gloom. A massive spider, crouched in regal stillness, draped so heavily in spider silk that she mistook it at first for another intrusion of the great roots of the forest. She froze in fear, the lowest precincts of her brain understanding that she was a prey animal, existing to feed creatures like this.

But it was dead: a desiccated husk. It loomed before the pews, twice the size of an automobile. The nubs of unlit candles were arrayed around it, white with dust. Veronica stepped closer, feeling something like holy wonder. Despite its death, she felt the presence of a coiled power—radiating from the roots of the trees, from the spider's corpse, from the web-curtained darkness itself. It crawled over her skin with a million tiny legs.

The room continued beyond the altar, and she saw something moving there, close to the ground, at the edges of her candlelight. A voice carried to her, soft and sibilant, followed quickly by more, like a clutch of huddled people urgently whispering. Veronica crept forward, driven by an appalled curiosity. The adult in her had been subdued by violence and fear, and the little girl she used to be—the one who sang to the moon, who stared at its radiant eye each night and vowed to understand its mysteries—was in the ascendent.

The nimbus of candlelight first illuminated several pairs of human feet, bodies supine, being dragged slowly across the floor. She hesitated, reluctant to reveal anything further. The whispering welled from just beyond the light's reach. The feet were dragged another few inches into the dark, as though something clutched the hair of their corpses and dragged them over the stone. Veronica's heart fluttered, a small sound escaped her throat.

Moon, are you lonely?

She stepped forward, the candelabra held aloft.

Are you cold?

Six Alabaster Scholars were being dragged along on their backs, their heads breached at various points and joined together by a great knot of web—obscuring an eye here, the left side of a face there, but in each case leaving the whispering mouth free, so that this crawling monstrosity seemed to be conversing with itself. Huge, spidery legs—she counted five—extruded from the webby cluster joining their brains and pulled them along through the darkness like the train of a ghastly wedding dress.

The thing did not acknowledge her or the light she carried. It just kept crawling, its unintelligible whisper crowding all thought from her head. Where was this broken thing going? What did it want?

From the shadows beyond it she heard the sound of

something heavy being struck, followed by a sharp crack. She remembered the sound well from her days on the farm: it was the sound of butchery.

Dr. Cull emerged from the gloom. He stepped forward hesitantly, a dripping bone saw suspended from his right hand. His hair was unkempt and his eyes reflected the candlelight like pale discs. His white coat was splashed with blood.

"Mrs. Brinkley. What are you doing down here, you silly girl?"

Fear crashed through her. Forgetting the stitches, she tried to speak. She released a muted sound, and the pain silenced her.

Cull extended his left hand to her. It was the cleaner of the two. "You are very willful, do you know that? I see now why your husband brought you to me. Come here."

She stepped backward, nearly tripping over a tumble of broken stone. The candles guttered, and half of them went out.

He carried no light with him. How had he been able to see?

Another voice leeched from the darkness behind her. "Cut her up, Doctor. Cut her up and let them feed."

Grub. His heavy accent sounded almost soothing, and she could hear the hard logic of his suggestion. It was difficult to listen to a voice like that and not think it was a good idea. He shuffled across the border of her light, a gaudy maggot, his own fine clothes torn and rumpled by whatever had happened down here. He held his filthy hatchet in his left hand. He stared at her as he might a rat in the pantry.

"They won't eat her," said Dr. Cull. "Soma has betrayed me. He put something into her brain."

Veronica tried to speak again. She had to say something on her own behalf, something to stay whatever was about to happen to her. Or maybe she only needed to scream in rage. She wasn't sure which. There was simply a guttural howl that needed to be given voice.

"No, Mrs. Brinkley. You have exhausted my patience, just as you did your husband's. You will never speak again. Nothing you have to say matters at all." And then, "Kill her, Charlie."

He took a step closer to her, and she backed up, bumping into Grub, who blew out her candles with one rancid breath.

It's all right, Moon.

She managed to run a few feet before she tripped over a root and landed hard on her chin. She stretched her right hand into darkness, looking for something she could hold on to, something she could use to pull herself back to her feet. There was nothing.

I love you.

She heard the whisper of the hatchet parting the air, but she did not feel it bite into the crown of her skull. By the time it came down again, she felt nothing at all.

You can live with me.

IV.

Charlie Duchamp

At forty-four years of age, Charlie Duchamp made his living breaking bones for Goodnight Maggie, matriarch of a low-rent crime outfit fighting for its share of scraps at the Brooklyn docks. He was good at the work and he enjoyed it. He'd been raised in violence, and to Charlie it functioned as a kind of language, one through which he could communicate the purest expressions of his heart. The world operated according to rules which were opaque to him; watching Maggie navigate the complexities of her criminal operation both awed him and reminded him of his own intellectual limitations. Sometimes this caused an accumulation of great, wrathful emotion. Hurting people made it better, at least for a little while. Doing it for Maggie meant he could do it often, and with license.

Charlie would have spent the rest of his life in this happy

pursuit, pushing on until the inevitable day when someone would put a bullet through his head and spill his body into the harbor, except he'd lost control of himself the night he visited the Irishman in his home and killed him when he wasn't supposed to. The one unsanctioned murder in itself might not have damned him, but the thrill of it gave him a red eye and he killed the Irishman's wife and children, too, all five of them, and if that wasn't bad enough he also killed Crying Joey, who Maggie had sent with him as backup, when Joey tried to stop him.

Sitting at the Irishman's blood-spattered kitchen table afterward, Charlie allowed himself a few minutes to calm down and catch his breath, after which he placed a call to Maggie and told her what he'd done. Then he waited patiently for her men to arrive. When they got there—four of them, all armed—they found him sitting passively, staring at the wall, like a machine that had been turned off.

"Christ, Charlie. Maggie ain't happy with you, and you know how she gets. Why didn't you just run?"

"I'm no runner," was all he said.

Two hours later he was standing before her desk in the little warehouse where she conducted her business, fully expecting to pay for his little frolic with his life.

But he'd seen Maggie angry—it wasn't overt or theatrical; it was cold and quiet. More than one hapless fool had reckoned himself safe only moments before horror consumed his world. And she wasn't angry. She was sad.

Grieving. And this scared him more than her wrath, because this he could not understand.

"Poor Charlie," she said, touching his cheek. "It was always so hard for you."

The touch of her hand to his face was like a burning mark. He felt it long after she took it away, was consumed by it as she dismissed the men who'd brought him in.

"What should I do with you?" she said.

He didn't respond. He thought the answer was obvious.

"I knew your daddy. Did you know that?"

"No." Mention of his father recalled to him what he'd done to the Irishman and his family. He was not troubled by it.

"My daddy bought meat from him at his stall. Sometimes I came with. I was in love with all the different knives. I never knew there were so many kinds." She thought for a moment, staring at him. "He was a bad man, your father."

Charlie said nothing. This was obvious, too.

"I've always liked you, Charlie. You took a bad hand and made something out of it. You were my favorite, you know. I told you to do a job, there was no question it would get done."

He nodded. He could still feel her touch on his face.

"I'm going to help you. All right? There's a man I know. I think maybe he can fix you."

"Fix me how?" He knew there was something wrong but he did not think it was in himself. He thought it was in the world.

"I don't want you to ask questions. I want you to do what I tell you. Just like always. All right?"

"Yes."

What Charlie did not know was that Goodnight Maggie had known and worked with a surgeon once local to the area, whose name was Barrington Cull. She trafficked in moon silk, among other things, and he became one of her most ardent customers. In time they contrived an arrangement by which Cull provided medical attention to people brought to him after hours in exchange for living subjects—usually people she wanted disappeared, but not always—for his brain experiments, in which the silk was apparently a vital component. He did all this under the guise of treating depressives, and he'd achieved enough success with wealthy patrons that he'd been able to parlay it into establishing the Barrowfield Home for Treatment of the Melancholy. Though this necessarily brought their professional relationship to an end, she couldn't help but feel a certain maternal pride. And if all the strange work the Cull boy had done on people who once suffered at Charlie's hand would now provide the key for healing Charlie's own demented brain, and return a favorite employee to reliable function besides, well—Maggie always did appreciate a bit of symmetry.

They strapped him down like a psychotic for the duration of his trip to the moon, but such measures were unnecessary. After the exertion of his last escapade, Charlie was as docile as a lamb. He felt chastened by Maggie's dismissal, and he couldn't decide whether her decision to spare his life was a mark of honor or a badge of shame. Furthermore, her touch continued to warm his cheek. As always with him, confusion was the seed of violence, and though he felt calm as he stared at the rounded metal roof over his head, his be-wilderment would exact a toll in blood sometime soon.

Or: it would have. But the young and ambitious Dr. Cull was experiencing some difficulties of his own. When this gift-wrapped package of directionless brutality arrived at the landing, he received it as a sign of the cosmos submitting itself to the force of his will.

"The cosmos is only as we perceive it," he told Charlie one night, almost a year later, as they sipped brandy during a quiet evening in the Sanctuary. Charlie did not like brandy but he drank it because Dr. Cull gave it to him. "Change the way you think of it, and you will change the very structure of time and space." Blood crusted the underside of Charlie's fingernails. He rarely troubled to wash his hands after one of his excursions into the tunnels, and Dr. Cull never made an issue of it.

He was here to help keep patients in line, but mostly he was here to kill the Alabaster Scholars. There was one good one, who assisted Dr. Cull in his treatments. The rest were bad. They didn't like that the doctor built his hospital over their crypt, they didn't like that he went down into the tunnels, and they liked it even less that he was using the spider silk in his surgeries. He didn't know what they were down there for; the Moon Spider was dead. To hear the doctor tell it, *all* the Moon Spiders were dead. So what did those bastards care? Why were they here at all? It was a pleasure to kill them.

"For example, I take a memory from one patient's mind and sew it into another's. Does it matter to the second patient that the memory isn't theirs—is, as they might say, false? No, it does not. For them, the new memory is as real as if it had actually happened to them. As far as they're concerned, it *did* happen. Their cosmos has been changed. If you take a weak mind and graft a strong memory into it, the patient's moral strength will be bolstered in kind. I have conducted experiments of this sort already and the results have been surprising, sometimes even amusing. But always life-changing.

"Now, what of those post-surgical patients who report of the occasional vision, glimpses into the starry gulf? Alien landscapes? What to make of them, Charlie?

"It makes me wonder. What if the old legend about the moon contains a kernel of truth? What if the moon is the remnant of some ancient being, all its exotic memories archived in the webs, tended to by the spiders? The Alabaster Scholars are trying to hatch a new Moon Spider. Their grotesque failures infest the tunnels beneath us. But why do they want this? Is it because the Spiders might awaken what sleeps? Or, if it's dead—call to another?"

Charlie stared at him impassively.

"I have barely touched upon what is possible. If we can incorporate some of this being's mind into our own minds with the spider silk, Charlie—imagine the possibilities. We could do anything we wanted. You could fold time like a handkerchief and step into your childhood home to tell your father what you really thought of him.

"Godhood is within our grasp."

Charlie tried hard to concentrate. He didn't understand

these cosmic things, but he liked the idea of going back to confront his father. It seemed like dime magazine stuff though, and he was reluctant to believe it, despite the doctor's intelligence. And anyway if it was true, why was Dr. Cull putting the special webs into other people, and not himself?

These things were not for him to ponder. Charlie knew two things. One: he was here to kill the Alabaster Scholars, and that meant going down into the tunnels, with the webs and the altars and the strange creatures connected by their brains—relics of the Scholars' own bizarre experiments, which he did not care to know about. It wasn't like the work he did in New York, but in the end all bodies come apart in the same ways. And two: if he did his job well enough, the doctor would cure him, and he could go home to Goodnight Maggie. It was the only thing driving him.

"Don't forget your promise, Doctor."

Dr. Cull, lost in some starry reverie, blinked and looked at him. "What did you say?"

"You made a promise."

"I know I did, Charlie. I haven't forgotten."

"I don't want to be sick. I want you to take out the rotten part, like you did for the others. So I can go back to work for Maggie. When I kill all the Scholars, then you'll fix me." Charlie had always found it useful to remind people of their obligations in simple terms. That way there would be no doubt of the reason if he had to punish them later.

Cull leaned back in his chair, and he got the look on his face that Charlie hated so much. Disappointed. Impatient.

The look his father had gotten all the time, when Charlie was little. The look that preceded terrible actions.

"You're useful to me, Charlie. You have *use*. Just like you did with Maggie. But for something so much bigger. Isn't that important to you?"

Sometimes Maggie would get that look, too. But then he would do whatever she told him to do, and it would go away, and he'd feel something funny in his chest that he guessed was probably love. If he said the right thing here, maybe he could make the look on the doctor's face go away, too.

"Yes it is," he said.

Dr. Cull kept staring at him, his expression unchanged. "But you miss her, don't you."

Charlie felt the sting of tears. He nodded, lowering his head in shame.

"You poor, stupid ape. You just want to be loved." Dr. Cull's eyes unfocused, and he seemed to drift away a moment. He finished his brandy and set the snifter on the table at his side. "You're right, Charlie. I've been unfair. I promised to help you, and I will. And perhaps I'll find something in that marvelous head of yours that will help someone else in days to come. Tomorrow morning, it will be *you* in the treatment room. We'll take care of your problem once and for all."

***

The next morning, while Charlie was anesthetized, Dr. Cull opened the top of his head and began removing large portions of his brain. Cull removed his yearning for love, his self-reflection, his hopes for a return to New York and to Maggie's good graces. He left in place the brutality and the desire to serve. He made Charlie Duchamp, as much as he was able, into an extension of his own will: a clenched fist; a grip at the throat. The tame Scholar at his side dropped in a handful of tiny spiders along with a smear of web harvested from the outskirts of the forest. The spiders had already begun their construction when Cull clamped the top of the skull back into place. In a matter of hours Charlie Duchamp was a new creature, his brain made whole by their labors.

The spiders were necessary to return the brain to its shape. The webs, as Cull hypothesized, acted as neural conductors. The hope was that the personality left behind would expand to fill the reconstructed brain. Sometimes there were complications: something fundamental to the brain's mechanism was compromised by the process and the patient never regained consciousness; sometimes the ancient memories in the thoughts contained by the web overwhelmed the mind, and the patient awoke driven mad by the visions of an immeasurable alien mind. When successful, though, the webbing filled the brain's missing places with minimal side effects. And so the remainder of Charlie's brain combined with the rags of an older intelligence, and for the rest of his life Charlie's dreams were seasoned with memories of a dead colossus: the ice seas of Europa, the storm-cities of Neptune, the mausoleum ships drifting beyond the solar system's edge.

The following day Cull led Charlie to the top of Barrowfield Home, where a small satellite was affixed to a rocket aimed into the gulf overhead. The satellite was small and round, bristling with antennae and blinking lights. It looked like a giant, metallic sea urchin. Charlie felt a twinge of recognition when he saw it, though he had never encountered anything like this before in his life.

Around the Home the forest swayed in the quiet wind, the curtains of web flowing like banners.

"Say hello, Charlie."

"To what? To a metal ball?"

"To yourself."

Charlie felt suddenly ill. He knew then why he recognized it. He stepped forward, afraid to touch it, yet extending his fingers toward it anyway. The metal hull was cold.

"Inside the satellite is a jar with the part of your brain I removed. With more spiders, of course. A full, working brain. *Your* brain. Isn't it marvelous?"

"The rotten part."

"Well. The part you don't need anymore."

Charlie circled the satellite, his eyes glittering in the starlight. He felt afraid of this thing, and fear made him angry. "I don't like this," he said. "Why are you doing it."

"Remember when I told you the other night about how the moon might be the remains of an ancient being?"

Charlie did not think that a question worth answering.

"There are other moons, Charlie. What if they're like this one? What if our planets are surrounded by dead gods and all their hidden knowledge? What if they're still alive? What are they doing? What are they for? How can we use them? I'm sending a part of your brain to find out. And if you find it, you'll use that new knowledge to come back and tell me."

Charlie didn't understand. He had no interest in finding anything alive, out there or anywhere at all, except that he might be allowed to kill it. Life was noxious to him. He wasn't a fool; he had a pretty good idea of what Cull had done to him. The desire for reunification with Maggie was gone, along with the longing for any human touch. Instead he wished only to practice the art he had spent so many years perfecting. He was interested to discover that the impulse to kill the half of himself locked in the satellite was particularly strong. Idly, he considered the strength it would take to incapacitate Dr. Cull long enough to smash the hide of the satellite and pry himself out—the mewling, compromised version of himself, the part that needed love and had love yet to give; the rotten part of the meat—and grind it beneath his heel. He wondered if he would hear himself scream.

Time to stall the urge before he did something terrible. He sought the memory of his father, the one where he appeared in the hall with the dead pig over his shoulders, which always made him small and quiet. Until the end, and then it made him feel strong and satiated.

But it wasn't there.

He waited for an emotion to rise in answer to this mysterious absence—anger, fear, confusion—but there was only a frustrating and unanswerable emptiness. More importantly, a murder he had done—his favorite one, as fundamental to his identity as his own face—was gone. It had been cored from his head like a bruise from an apple, and he had nothing left but the memory of its shape. And even as he acknowledged this, that memory too began to fade.

"Where is my murder?" he said.

Dr. Cull smiled and took him by the elbow. "We're launching soon," he said. "This will be the first of many explorations. We can watch it from the garden if you'd like. Afterward, I'll fill you with murders."

Cull certainly tried. But Charlie had an appetite beyond his imagining.

***

Now, two years later, the woman was dead and everything had gone wrong. Grub hurried down the long hall of Wing C. Candles had been lit by the staff to compensate for the cut power. His right knee was hurting. He felt his trousers tugging against it where the blood had turned tacky, and he wondered if he would lose the leg. Would he be of any use to the doctor with only one leg? He didn't see how. More immediately, he didn't see how he could continue his murderous campaign against the Scholars if he were hobbled. He might have to turn his attentions closer to home.

But that was a problem for later. For now, at least, Dr. Cull still required his services. The Alabaster Scholars were in open revolt. They had boiled up from below and infiltrated Barrowfield Home, moving silently in the shadows and picking off staff members when they could. Grub kept coming across bodies, some butchered like animals, others with their skin swollen and dark, as if they'd been poisoned.

As if these Scholars had taken on the properties of spiders themselves.

How many of them could there be? The Home was built over the grave of just one Moon Spider, and Grub had been methodically killing them since he'd arrived. It must be that the tunnels were all interconnected, that there was a labyrinthine subterranean network interlocking all the graves throughout all the moon, and they were all here to make their stand against the doctor.

They had never hurt Grub before. They had never even tried.

He reached the end of the wing and pushed through a pair of swinging doors into a cramped, cold room. Corpse-laden gurneys lined the walls on either side; opposite the doors was a work table burdened with tall pieces of machinery connected by thick, opaque tubing. Several cloudy jars suspended from the machine, shedding a misty glow into the morgue's low light. Grub dragged a heavy table before the door, providing a dubious protection.

Dr. Cull was already there. On one of the gurneys, pulled away from the others, lay Veronica Brinkley, her hands and her shift covered in blood, her lips still stitched closed, and her skull—once neatly opened for the surgeries—now cloven like a fruit. The doctor was fixing metal rods into the top of her head. They looked like radio antennae, recalling the satellite he'd launched from the roof containing a portion of Grub's own brain.

Grub paused. She was the one who'd given him his new name. He said it again to himself, feeling the word in his mouth: a heavy syllable, like a smooth stone. "Grub." It had a warm sound. It made him think of soil, of Earth. It helped to divide himself from who he used to be. It told him he might become something new.

He hadn't thought about this when he brought the hatchet down onto her head—Dr. Cull had made him something new, too, something simple and clean—but he'd thought about it often since. With each Alabaster Scholar he caught lurking in the corridors, with each life he stole and each corpse he left in his wake, he thought about his new name. He was starting to feel confused again.

Cull stopped what he was doing. "Charlie," he said, using the wrong name. "For God's sake, it's about time."

"I was ambushed in the hall," Grub said. "They slashed my knee."

The doctor gave no sign that he'd heard him.

"Come here. Hold this. We have to be quick."

Grub positioned himself on the other side of the gurney and grasped one of the metal rods, holding it still while Dr. Cull adjusted its anchoring in the brain.

"She's dead, Doctor. The Scholars are coming up from underground. We don't have time for this. We have to fortify the door."

"Just do what I say, God damn you."

"They're going to kill us."

Cull backhanded him, hard. Grub's head rocked back, the shock of it greater than the pain. Behind them, the Scholars had reached the door, pounding steadily.

"Listen to me, Charlie. Soma was a traitor. He put something in her head in the last treatment. They're trying to make another one. We have to burn it out. We have to get it out before it's too late. He was working against me the whole time. The whole time! *Why?*"

Charlie looked into Mrs. Brinkley's head. The two rods were wedged tight, one leaning to the front, the other canted to one side. One of them trailed a thin wire, ready to be hooked into some kind of a machine. The doctor hadn't been trying to transfer her brain into a satellite; he was trying to burn it out. Even as Grub watched, spiders swarmed over it, wrapping it in a cocoon of web like a fat, bloody fly. Little filigrees of web connected the two rods, as though they were twigs on a tree.

Nestled in the meat of the brain, exposed by the fissure Grub had dug with his hatchet, was a thick, pale egg sac, larger than any he had ever seen. And he'd seen many in the tunnels.

An awareness of impending doom settled over him. He didn't understand what was happening, which was not unusual. But it was plain that neither did the doctor, and that was something new. He looked back to the door, which was beginning to splinter beneath the Scholars' onslaught. A great machine was turning, one beyond either of them, and it was about to grind them both in its teeth. The prospect elated him. Here at last would be the great shedding of blood he had craved his whole life, a tide of it to overwhelm him and reshape the world. Here would be the flourishing of his art. None of this was to be stopped.

As Dr. Cull worked to fix the wire to an electrical generator—to burn the egg sac where it nestled—Grub casually took the doctor's right arm and snapped it at the elbow.

Cull screamed. He dropped to the floor in agony, cradling his arm to his side. The table at the door scraped over the floor as the Alabaster Scholars pushed through, their own white robes now splashed with gore, their pale faces dappled and lined.

Veronica convulsed once, her hands scrabbling at the sides of the gurney, one leg kicking, then shuddering into stillness. And then she sat up.

V.

Nebraska

Veronica and her mother were nearly finished tidying the kitchen, and she was dreading the walk to fetch water. Getting to the well was easy enough, but hauling the heavy, sloshing pails back inside without spilling too much hurt her arms terribly. Outside, her father was stabling the mule, and her brothers had already been dispatched to the stream, where they were allowed to bathe. She didn't know why she should be made to carry the pails when they were taller and stronger, and already done with their work.

And when she came back, there was still the laundry to soak.

"Stop woolgathering, girl, and get back to work." Her mother was whisking the broom over the floor, which Veronica thought a futile task: the boys would only bring more dirt inside, and she'd have to start all over again. And then again tomorrow. And again the next day.

"It isn't fair," she said.

Her mother stopped, a beleaguered expression on her face. "Now, that's a fine word," she said.

"The boys are at the stream already."

"Well, they're boys. They get to do lots of things you don't get to do. You might as well get used to it."

Veronica sighed, impatient with the conversation already. She glanced out the window and saw her father drop the latch over the barn door. Overhead, the sky shaded from orange at the world's rim to a dark, bruised purple. The first stars began to peer out.

"I'm going to the moon when I get older," she said, looking for it overhead. "I told Father and he agreed."

The sweeping came to a stop. Veronica turned and saw that her mother's face had hardened. "Your father tells you pretty dreams because he thinks girls need them. They don't. What they need is the truth. When you get older you're going to marry a man—with means, if we're at all lucky—and make a family. And God help you if you ever become a burden to them."

Veronica hated it when her mother spoke like this. She must derive some perverse joy from being hateful, she thought. It only made her want to escape this house the more.

"How could I ever become a burden to them? That doesn't make any sense."

"When what you need outweighs what you offer. Make no mistake, child. Your life does not belong to you."

Veronica turned her back on her mother and put her face to the window, where the air was cool and true darkness was settling over the land. "That's *your* life, Mama. It won't be mine."

She knew it was an awful thing to say but she didn't feel bad about saying it. Nevertheless, she was careful not to look at her mother's reflected face in the window.

"God help you, if what you say is true."

Veronica turned. "Why, Mama?"

"Because if you're going to take your life for your own you'll have to give up everything else. Do you understand me? It will cost you so much it breaks my heart to even think about it."

Veronica did not understand. She only knew that her mother seemed determined to ruin her dreams. Maybe she wanted her daughter to be miserable because she was so miserable herself. Veronica scowled through the window again. She watched her father putting tools back in their place. She wanted to be out there with him. He believed in her.

"Go on then," her mother said, disappointment plain in her voice. "Go outside with him, for as long as he'll have you. I'll fetch the water."

"Really?" She turned, suspicious of the unexpected generosity. She was alarmed to see her mother hastily wiping away a tear.

"I said so, didn't I?"

"Mama? Did I do something wrong?"

"Not you. Go on now."

And so Veronica dashed out to join her father under the

night sky, where they watched the faraway streaks of light as the rockets slipped away from the world.

"Tell me a story about the moon," she said.

She watched it sail through the rushing clouds, lighting them up from the inside like huge gray lanterns. And it seemed to her that it watched her right back, as though it had been waiting all this time for her to come outside and say hello. As though it knew her so well it might call her by her name.

***

Veronica stands alone in the early morning, dragging the ax through the dirt. The sun will breach the horizon soon, but for now it's still dark. The moon is a pale crescent. She is small, and the ax is heavy.

She remembers a younger sister she never had, who liked to ride on her shoulders. Veronica once took her all the way across the Brooklyn Bridge so they could watch the boats pass underneath.

I've never seen the Brooklyn Bridge . . .

Something was wrong with her sister's bones, though, and it made her cry. It was hard to listen to. Mother fretted over her sister's body, which pain had twisted into an ugly shape. She would have been quiet if she'd been able to. It wasn't her fault.

Father got so angry sometimes. He worked around noise all the time and he didn't like it noisy at home, too. It made his brain hurt.

Veronica walked up the porch steps and pushed the door open, stepping into a hallway she'd never seen before. A sound drifted toward her. A small, stifled cry of distress. The hallway was close and hot. The noise of traffic thrummed beyond it, a city noise, a noise she had not experienced until much later in her life, when she moved East to live with her husband. The hallway terminated at an open door, and in the room beyond it was her little sister, lying in bed. Her limbs were bending in on themselves. Her face was flattened in terrible concentration. Mother sat beside her, wiping her forehead with a cloth.

"Ssssh, baby. Stay quiet, please stay quiet." She looked over her shoulder and saw Veronica standing in the doorway. Her face buckled in fury. *"Charlie, shut the door!"* she hissed.

Veronica backed out, closing the door. A powerful grief moved through her body, weird and rough-edged, an unfamiliar feeling of focused pain. She was accustomed to something more nebulous: floating, existential, sourceless. This was different. This was like a spade digging into the heart's earth.

"I just want quiet," said somebody behind her, and she turned to see her father treading wearily up the stairs. A pig was slung over his shoulders, a carcass he'd brought home from work. It was an alarming sight. He did his butchering at the shop; there was no reason to bring home the whole animal. It was the first and mildest sign that something had gone wrong in his head. His hands clenched and unclenched, as though he were trying one last time to find something he might grasp hold of before falling. He walked past her as though he didn't see her; and maybe he didn't.

He pushed his way into the room Veronica had just backed out of, affording her another quick glimpse of mother and child, their eyes fixed with terror. "I just want a moment's peace," he said, and closed the door, leaving Veronica on the other side.

Screams blossomed in the air. She ran, shame twisting her gut. *You ran away. You're a runner, that's what you are.* She half-collapsed down the stairs, clutching the bannister to keep from tumbling down altogether. She dashed into the storage closet beneath the stairs, pulled the hanging coats closed like a curtain, and tried not to breathe. The screams were already over. She heard his footsteps clomping heavily back down the stairs. They sounded like the sky booming over her head. He called for her.

"Charlie," he said. "Where are you, boy."

"You're not my daddy," she whispered. "I want my real daddy."

Pressing herself further back in the closet, her fingers brushed over the wooden haft of an ax.

The closet door opened.

She was standing over her parents, sprawled in their bed. Her hands were sweaty around the raised ax. They were awake now, staring at her.

"I'm sorry," she said. "This isn't me. This isn't my memory."

Her mother's face had the same expression she'd worn in the kitchen that distant morning: melancholy; angry, but not at her. "Claim it," she said.

And so she did. Mother first, because she was the stronger of the two, unbeguiled by pretty dreams.

Her father covered his eyes. He looked like a little boy.

(runner)

"Piglet?" he said.

And she claimed it again.

Her brothers were sleeping in the loft. She felt a terrible guilt as she made the climb, but it dissipated even as she acknowledged it. In its place there came a new element: something cold and clean, something strong and terrible.

The loft was choked with webs. It overwhelmed everything, as though it were a kind of atmosphere, a gauzy Heaven. And there was God, a hulking black shape obscured by white cotton candy wisps, as big as a wagon. His eight legs arched and thin, His mandibles twitching. He extended one foreleg to her and all of Heaven thrummed and shook. She saw her own blood spatter the pale web, a shock of color in all that white; she felt it running down her face in little red rivulets from where her brain lay exposed to His faceted eye.

***

Veronica awoke to bedlam. Violence filled the morgue: Grub swung whatever lay to hand at the Alabaster Scholars descending upon him. They clutched at his clothing and grasped at his face, even as one and then another fell beneath his bludgeoning hands. Dr. Cull was dragged screaming into the hallway's dark gullet, one arm jauntily cocked where his elbow had been broken, as though he were waving a cheerful goodbye. As he was pulled beyond her sight, the sound he made could have been mistaken for laughter.

She swung her feet off the gurney, planted them onto

cold stone. She stepped across the blood-slicked floor. The
Scholars immediately stopped their struggles and dropped
to their knees. Grub staggered to the wall, exhausted. His
hands were raw, the knuckles bleeding. He looked at her,
his face without expression, fighting to catch his breath. She
directed the Scholars to take him. She did not need to speak
it, only to think it.

To Grub she thought, *Be still,* and he was.

They led him through the darkened hallways, over the
sprawled bodies of the dead. Those who were still living
she directed be brought with them. Wall-mounted candles
guided the way.

Many of the patients had been freed from their cells.
Some she encountered wandering the halls stunned and
lost; some ran with purpose, though to what destination
they couldn't know; and some lay in slaughtered heaps.
Those who saw her gave her a wide berth, or fled outright.

She didn't blame them. She knew how she looked, pass-
ing through the little islands of light: pale, wrapped in a
thin and bloody gown, her mouth sewn shut in rough, ugly
jags. A thick spiderweb stretched between the two metal
prongs extending from her cloven head. She looked like a
monster herself. Like some horrible lab experiment crawled
from its jar, lurching hungrily through the dark.

The thought filled her with an emotion so alien to her
experience, it took her some time to recognize it as joy.

She did not worry about the ones who ran. They would
all be collected eventually.

Veronica and the Scholars mounted a curving bank of

stairs and reached the second floor, eventually entering the room the doctor called the Sanctuary. The candles were not lit in here, but one of the Alabaster Scholars detached from the group and attended to them, until the room flowered into a shivering, golden radiance. The ranks of books towered over them, with narrow windows between the shelves looking out onto the vast forest, like slices of cool blue light.

Grub looked around the room, and a calm seemed to settle over him. Not the calm she had forced on him, but one emerging from his own experiences of this room. So it was a place of safety for him, too, as it was meant to be for her and for all of Dr. Cull's patients.

Her head felt heavy and unwieldy. She had to put her hand against one of the bookshelves to keep from falling over. Titles leapt out at her: *Leechcraft and the Mechanism of the Soul. The Philosophy of the Wretched.* What an unmusical thing, to be a human being. She had a nagging memory of something grander, buried in the human meat of her brain. It rolled over, struggling to be recalled.

The egg sac in her brain split open, and hundreds of tiny spiders erupted. They crawled up the web between the rods, spilled onto her gown, dropped to the floor. A gorgeous warmth cascaded through her body; her blood felt incandescent. The feeling of physical disorientation faded. Three long, spindly legs—each as long as her own arm—emerged from her brain, flexing in luxurious freedom, arcing over her head like a living crown. She saw their shadow thrown onto the floor, backlit by a bank of candles, and she felt like Medusa in her lair.

Hang him, she thought. And the Scholars lifted Grub against the wall, mounting him there with webs hidden amid their white robes, stitching him in place with long needles. *Hang them all.*

"What's happening?" he said. He tried to push one of the Scholars away, but there was no strength to it. "No. No. This isn't what I want."

Be calm, she told him again, and his weak struggles ceased. But his eyes communicated confusion and fear. Within minutes he was cocooned to the wall. As she watched, surviving staff members were dragged in to be mounted beside him. They would serve a noble purpose, for once in their horrid little lives; food would be needed. Patients were brought in, too, but they would have another fate. The Scholars would tend to them later, as Veronica herself had been tended to. But this time they would do it under her guidance.

A thought occurred to her, almost too small to entertain, certainly a petty remnant of an earlier life: her husband. He would be at home now, in a study which looked much like this one, reclining in a chair by the fire, eyes sliding over the newsprint of the evening edition. Too small a matter for her now, yes, but not for the Scholars who served her. In the corner stood Soma, good and faithful Soma, his right arm severed above the elbow and his gown splashed with blood, his own and his many victims'. She summoned him and he approached gladly. Then she stepped closer to the webs with which the Scholars had begun to coat the library walls, and with a small pinch and twist of her forelegs—*like folding a handkerchief,* Cull had said, though not to her—she created an opening. Soma stepped through and emerged into her husband's study, in a shadowed corner of the room across from the chair where he rested.

Her husband lowered his paper, his brow creased. "Hello? Hello, is someone there?"

Veronica allowed herself the small pleasure of watching his face blanch when Soma emerged from the shadows, a blood-steeped ghost, there to do the work of spiders upon him. Then she turned away, because there was no more space for her husband in her thoughts.

Content, she left the Scholars to their labors. She would revisit this room when it was refitted to her liking.

She passed through the hallways, down the stairs, until she reached the vast reception area where her husband first signed her over to Barrowfield—a once holy site perverted into a factory of derangement and disease. She would make it holy again. The receptionist lay face down in the middle of the foyer, as if placed there like a piece of art.

Beyond, the front doors gaped wide. Veronica stepped outside by her own choice for the first time since her arrival. The gardens stretched before her, dotted with the few patients who had yet to be corralled. The fountain gushed against the black gulf of the sky. A crescent Earth glimmered above. Further down the walk stood the vacant landing pad. No shuttle would land there again.

Around Barrowfield Home, the forest writhed, branches heaving and wood splintering in a ferocious wind. The dense canopy of web was being torn from its moorings, drifting down to the forest's interior or lifting like sails carried off into the night.

Bentley was there, on his customary bench at the fountain's base. He did not seem shocked by Veronica's appearance. It was a time of transformations, after all.

"I've never seen the forest like this," he said, as if they had joined for their usual conversation. And then his face crumpled in grief. "I wanted to live. Isn't that stupid? It turns out, after all, I wanted to live."

Veronica touched Bentley's head, where the incision was red and the stitches were loose. Spiders crawled from beneath her sleeve, down her hand, and disappeared into the incision. *You will,* she said.

She kept walking. She did not spare another glance for Bentley, who would be taken into the dark, glaring façade of Barrowfield Home and turned to his new purpose. She did not spare another thought for her husband, who was by now suffering in ways unfathomable even to a practitioner of the surgeon's arts. Instead she felt a swelling of joy on behalf of all the imprisoned melancholy, all of whom would live, all of whom would become hosts to great populations. Soon these cold and ghostly forests would throng with life once again, and the moon would open its glaring eye.

She dropped to her knees, fell to her hands, and sloughed off her old body altogether. She ran on new legs with a breathtaking, joyous speed. She launched into the branches and into the webs, where she heard the tolling of the outer planets and felt the great, booming currents of the stars.

Running across the tops of the trees, she turned her eye to the blue and green sliver of Earth. She peered down through the long gulf until she found the little girl staring back up at her, a flag of life in the blowing wheat.

ACKNOWLEDGMENTS

I owe gratitude to so many. To Dale Bailey, to whom this story is dedicated, for his patience and encouragement in reading multiple drafts of this novella throughout its composition; to Lisa Nance for lighting a fire under my butt to get this done, when my faith in it was floundering; to Matthew Bartlett and Scott Dorward for reading early drafts; to Dan Chaon, Paul Tremblay, Laird Barron, Seanan McGuire, and Owen King for their kind endorsements; to my wonderful agent Renée Zuckerbrot and her associate Anne Horowitz at MMQLIT for more than I can express in a line; to Ellen Datlow, Irene Gallo, Matt Rusin, Debbie Friedman, Sam Araya, Christine Foltzer, Jordan Hanley, Valeria Castorena, Khadija Lokhandwala, and the rest of the team at Tor Nightfire (I'm thrilled to be joining the family); to Daniel Carpenter and his team at Titan Books in the UK; and to Anna Carmichael and her colleagues at Abner Stein. All of these people put work into this book, and all share a portion of whatever good qualities it might have.

Last on this list but first in importance, thanks go to my daughter, Mia, for acting as a soundboard as I worked out ideas, for being free with her good advice, and for being kind and patient with a moody and distracted old man. I appreciate it more than you can ever know, kiddo.

***

Okay, there is one more person. Thank you, reader, for trusting me once again. None of it means a damn without you.

READ ON FOR A PREVIEW OF
BOOK 2 IN THE LUNAR GOTHIC TRILOGY

CATHEDRAL OF THE DROWNED

Available August 2025 from Tor Books

I.

Red Hook, 1924

On the night they dragged Handsome Billy from the harbor, his belly slit from cock to rib cage and his innards spilling out like wet fish, Goodnight Maggie came home to a ghost from her past, the man in the moon she thought long dead. He crouched by the steps to her brownstone, hidden so well in the shadows that she would have missed him entirely had he not stood to present himself after her driver pulled away.

It was four in the morning. Clouds scudded across the sky. Rain had threatened all day but there had been nothing but a cold, driving wind. She'd just come back from the docks, where Billy's corpse had been discovered in a fishing net dropped in front of McElhone's Fishery, the warehouse from which she ran a gang that, until a few months ago, had run the docks in Red Hook with uncontested dominance.

They handled booze, gambling, and prostitutes; but what kept them in control was their exclusive access to moonsilk.

Then the Italians started arriving, and with them came a new organization calling themselves the Mafia. They were hungry and strong, and they wanted what she had. Handsome Billy—seventeen years old, a sweet child with a useful mean streak—was meant to make that clear.

So when a youngish, disheveled man, who years ago had been one of her most ardent customers, lurched unexpectedly from the shadows in front of her house, she nearly put a bullet through his head from simple reflex. If she hadn't been numb with cold and so tired that her eyes burned, he wouldn't have had time to speak.

"Maggie," he said. "It's me."

She recognized the voice, even after all this time. "Come out where I can see you." The gun did not leave her hand.

The figure shuffled closer, until the lamp across the street illuminated the face of Doctor Barrington Cull.

It no longer looked much like a face at all. The skin had been flayed or torn from the left side from the corner of his mouth over the crown of his head, leaving a pale, shiny mass of scar tissue which pulled his features askew. A hole gaped where his eye had been. He favored his left leg, which looked twisted under his threadbare pants. His clothes were rags: not torn and bloody, but grimy and ill-fitting. A vagrant's garb.

"I need help," he said.

Maggie slipped the gun back into her pocket. "I heard you were dead."

"Yes. I know."

"Did Charlie do this to you?"

Dr. Cull glanced furtively up and down the dark street, where the streetlamps shed cones of light. The shadows between them festered with possibilities. The neighbors' windows were all dark at this hour, but dawn was near. "Please, can we go inside? They're looking for me."

"Who are?"

"The Alabaster Scholars. She sent them."

Maggie didn't know what that meant but it hardly mattered. She didn't want to be outside any longer either. "Can you walk on that leg?"

"These injuries are old. I'm fine."

"Then come on." She mounted the steps, unlocked the door, and ushered him inside. She hadn't realized how tense she'd been feeling until securing the locks again behind her. For the moment, she felt safe.

Goodnight Maggie lived alone. Though she had climbed a long way from being the poor little girl from the slums, she'd never been able to shake off the oppressive stink of failure, which lingered despite every hard-won block, every conquered rival, every new stratum of wealth. Her home was warm, her furniture was expensive, and art decorated her walls; yet she still spent each night steeped in the shame of poverty.

Dr. Cull followed her into the living room and stood uncertainly while she turned on a lamp and poured two glasses of Scotch whisky. She handed him one and pointed to a leather club chair. "Sit down, Barry."

A flicker of anger crossed his face. He hated when she called him that. But he said nothing as he took his seat. It struck her how different he seemed now. Seven years ago he'd been a brash young man—probably a genius, though she knew she was no judge of those things. But he'd been conducting experiments on the brains of the mad and the desperate in dingy little shacks along the wharf, using silk he bought from her, and after some trial and error the results became impressive enough that he was able to secure funding for the Barrowfield Home for the Melancholy, located offworld, near the forests of the moon.

That young man would have corrected her. "Barrington, if you please. Or simply, 'Doctor.'"

Not disrespectfully. Never that. Cull had always fancied himself a cultivated man; besides that, he needed her. He needed access to the silk, which she bought from two moon-runners, Little Frankie Delaware and his cousin Cy. They had a tiny rattle-trap ship which would take them to the moon and back, and they had the guts to venture into the forest to harvest the silk. The Moon Spiders were all supposed to be dead; nevertheless, people who went into the woods had a tendency not to come out again.

Maggie sat on her couch and leaned back, not even troubling to take off her coat. She closed her eyes, thoughts running amok.

The Italians had drawn first blood. She might have given them the booze and everything else, in the interests of survival—but not the silk. That was hers.

And Handsome Billy dead. Unforgivable. An outrage

that would have to be answered. Billy was a good boy who grew up without a mama and would do whatever Maggie told him to, as long as she treated him with a little kindness. No one is so easily steered as an unloved boy.

Thinking of Billy, as always, recalled Charlie Duchamp to her mind. Charlie was a man in his mid-forties when last she saw him in the flesh, nevertheless she still considered him one of her boys. One of her favorites. Yet he was unpredictably violent, and being unpredictable was a flaw. So she'd sent him to Cull to be fixed. And he never came back home.

Cull would have to answer for that.

She opened her eyes. Cull sat quietly in the chair, as docile as a choirboy. He took a greedy sip from his glass, then met her eyes.

"Thank me," she said.

"Thank you, Maggie."

"You made the papers here, almost a year ago. Your precious asylum taken over by the inmates. You and all your staff killed. Barrowfield out of business. The moon an expensive disaster, all travel there forbidden now."

He nodded, then seemed to change his mind, and shook his head. "That's not the real story."

"You've made things difficult for my moonrunners. Difficult for me. And just tonight the Italians killed one of my boys. There's going to be a war, and it's a war I don't think I can win. Now, on top of that, I have to deal with you, too?"

"Not for long. I just have to find a way to get off world."

"And go where?"

"Out there. As far as I can."

Maggie rubbed at her eyes. Thinking was difficult. She needed sleep. "Tell me about these students hunting you."

"Scholars," Cull said, a hint of impatience creeping into his voice. "The Alabaster Scholars. They worship the Moon Spiders. She's using them as assassins now."

Maggie didn't know who "she" was and would worry about that later. "They have their own spacecraft? They can find you here?"

"They don't need vessels. They can travel behind space now."

He was speaking nonsense. Maybe he was crazy. If so she could dispose of him easily enough. The Italians were her primary concern. If they found Frankie and his cousin they would take the silk trade from her. Now Barrington Cull created one more weak spot for her organization, one more point of entry for the Mafia.

She could not let him leave her apartment.

She put on her most reassuring voice; she assumed what she thought of as the mother mask. "I'll protect you, Barry."

He ducked his head. Tears of relief glistened in the low light. "I have to get back up there. I have to go out to the edge of the solar system. I have to see what's there. Will you help me do that too?"

"Of course. We have a lot to talk about. But right now we need to sleep. Take the guest bedroom. In the morning I'll have my boys bring you some fresh clothes. We'll figure out what to do, okay?"

"Yes. All right." He drained the last of his whisky. "It's been so long since I tasted anything like this."

"Have another if you like. It'll help you sleep."

He stood, a little shakily. "I won't need any help. I've been running from them. I haven't slept in two days." Halfway down the hall, he paused, and turned back to her. "Thank you, Maggie. I knew I could count on you. You're the only one on Earth I can."

She smiled. "Go to sleep, Barry. Everything will be okay."

Maggie poured herself another glass and sat there for a while longer. She was tired but her mind was spinning like an engine. Barrowfield fell apart a year ago. How long had Cull been back on Earth? What had he been doing? She was furious at this distraction but at the same time felt sure there was an opportunity here, something she could use in her war against the Mafia. She just had to get him to tell her everything, then study the problem. There'd never been a problem she couldn't think her way out of, never been an adversary she couldn't outwit.

She turned off the light and made her way down to her bedroom. She put her ear against the closed door of the guest room, until she could make out the slow, regular breathing of Cull, now fast asleep. Quietly she entered her own room and closed the door.

She undressed in the darkness, a soft city light coming in through the curtains. If the windows were open she'd be able to smell the salt in the air from the harbor. Slipping on her nightgown, she sat on the foot of her bed and faced the closet door, open only an inch or two.

Tomorrow would be full of anger and decisions and violence, and she desperately needed sleep, but more than that she needed to talk to him.

"Charlie? Are you there?"

She hated how much she needed to talk to him.

Silence.

"Charlie."

She heard the sound first, as always. A low static covering a nearly sub-audible hum, an electric whisper draped over a deep bass current. The hairs on her arms stood up. And then a pale light bled from inside her closet, the off-white of bone, flickering like a faulty bulb.

A few seconds later the door slowly opened. Standing in her closet was a wet, writhing form, a hulking humanlike shape which seemed in the ambient light to be composed of coiling worms, slugs, scuttling beetles. Atop this shape was a metal orb sprouting dozens of long silver spines in every direction. Some of them ended in red or blue blinking lights. A satellite. Oily water trickled from it in a series of steady streams, as if it rested beneath a small waterfall she could not see.

"There's my sweet boy," she said. This time she meant it.

"Hi, Maggie," Charlie said. "I've been waiting for you to come back."

"I'm sorry. I had to do a little business, but I'm back now."

"Good. I miss you when you're gone."

"Look above you, and tell me what you see."

The image flickered, and the satellite-head seemed to turn a fraction.

"Jupiter," he said. "It fills the whole sky. It's so beautiful. I wish you could see it."

She wiped at her eyes. She had to sleep so badly, but not yet. Not yet. "So do I," she said.

Outside, Earth's own moon glared in the sky.

A gibbous white shard.

A pitiless light.

ABOUT THE AUTHOR

NATHAN BALLINGRUD is the author of *The Strange, Wounds: Six Stories from the Border of Hell,* and *North American Lake Monsters: Stories,* which won the Shirley Jackson Award. He has been short-listed for the World Fantasy, British Fantasy, and Bram Stoker Awards. His stories have been adapted into the Hulu series *Monsterland.* He lives in Asheville, North Carolina.